SEBASTIAN

by Lawrence Durrell

NOVELS

The Avignon Quintet
Monsieur
Livia
Constance
Sebastian
Quinx

The Alexandria Quartet
Justine
Balthazar
Mountolive
Clea

The Revolt of Aphrodite
Tunc
Nunquam

The Black Book
The Dark Labyrinth

TRAVEL

Bitter Lemons
Reflections on a Marine Venus
Prospero's Cell
Sicilian Carousel
The Greek Islands

POETRY

Collected Poems
Selected Poems

DRAMA

Sappho

LETTERS AND ESSAYS

Spirit of Place edited by
Alan G. Thomas
Literary Lifelines: The Richard
Aldington–Lawrence Durrell
Correspondence

HUMOUR

Stiff Upper Lip
Esprit de Corps
Sauve Qui Peut

FOR YOUNG PEOPLE

White Eagles Over Serbia

ff

LAWRENCE DURRELL

Sebastian

or Ruling Passions

faber and faber
LONDON · BOSTON

First published in 1983
This edition first published in 1985
by Faber and Faber Limited
3 Queen Square London WC1N 3AU
Reprinted 1988

Printed in Great Britain by
Redwood Burn Limited, Trowbridge, Wiltshire

British Library Cataloguing in Publication Data

Durrell, Lawrence
Sebastian, or, Ruling Passions
I. Title
823.912 PR6007.U76
ISBN 0-571-13445-9

to Simone Périer
of Montaury by Nîmes

Contents

ACKNOWLEDGEMENTS

Thanks are hereby extended to Dr Torhild Leira who gave permission for the author to use hints from her beautiful article in the *International Review of Psychoanalysis*, vol. 7, pt 3, 1980, entitled 'The Release of Tears'.

ONE

The Recall

THE PRINCE WAS IN A VEXATION. HE HAD DECIDED ON the spur of the moment to return to Egypt with Affad whom he took to task very severely for having succumbed, as he put it, to the "whim" of falling in love with Constance. He pursued the theme doggedly as they rode in the official limousine towards the airport of Geneva. "It was completely *uncalled* for," he said, "in view of your superior experience and the *engagements* you had entered into with the seekers." He was referring to the small brotherhood of gnostics in Alexandria to which they both belonged and in the tenets of whose creed they both deeply believed. Yes, on this score Affad felt deeply guilty, deeply betrayed by his own desire. The face of Constance rose up in his memory as if to reproach him for what he could not help. "You had no *right* to fall in love," the Prince went on testily. "I will *not* have her hurt." Affad made an impatient noise in his throat. "There is no such thing, as you have said. We must find another word. I will not have *engouement*. It is something of another order. Not infatuation at all." (They were speaking French, their tone was high.) Then after a long silence Affad said, "The experience was new to me; I ran aground—*j'ai calé*. Prince, it was not myself acting. Besides, you talk as if you were in love with her yourself." This put the Prince into a fearful rage because it was true. He made a cryptic gobbling noise like an offended turkey and blew his nose in a cambric handkerchief.

The problem was insoluble. Surely the insidious goblins of love had ceased to exist on the thin moral fare offered by the modern world? Affad was thinking with deep desire mingled with remorse of that secret field or realm which constitutes the moral geography of the mystic. His friend Balthazar had once said ruefully, "I thought I was living my own life but all the time it was really living me without any extraneous aid. It had taken half a century for me to realise this! What a blow to my self-esteem!"

"Your behaviour is out of date," said the Prince again. "Since contraception things have changed. Women were once unique events in the life of a man; now woman is a mere commodity like *hay*. Availability has bred contempt."

"Not Constance!" he said.

"Of course Constance!" said the old man.

Affad thought back in silence. When he had first seen her he had been unable to believe his eyes, so original had her style of beauty seemed. ("I hate people acting out of epoch," said the Prince vehemently, and he intended the remark to wound.) "In fact so do I. But in any given moment of time some part of us is out of date, stays chronologically prehistoric in the most obstinate way. The kisses of ancestors take firm possession of our senses; we are mere distributors of love, not inventors. Even less investors."

"Fiddlesticks!" said the Prince.

"I was alarmed to find that for once this demonic sentiment was not moribund. I tried to escape it in vain, I really tried!"

"Fiddlesticks!" cried the Prince and gave a tiny stamp on the floor of the limousine. He was beside himself with . . . not only moral vexation but also jealousy. Affad said, "You are behaving as if I were a curate who had been untrue to his vows of chastity. I won't have it." But this was unfair, the business was much graver. It was in the most literal sense a matter of life and death and sacrifice. He had fallen short of his own intentions. In ancient times human sacrifice was invented to placate this particular demon. Think of the hundreds of imberb boys and impubert girls it had needed to placate the Cretan minotaur! "On my last birthday my old aunt Fatima sent me a telegram saying, 'Death is of no importance to It: why then to you?' Was she wrong?"

"Yes, she was wrong," said Affad, out of sheer contrariness, for the Prince was very annoying and there was no point in continuing to give in to him. On theological matters it was another affair – he would have to face the Star Chamber, so to speak, and answer for his fidelity; but this was an inner committee which had every right to probe his sincerity. They had never heard of Constance, like the Prince. "As a matter of fact Constance herself took a rather robust medical attitude to the sentiment you so much disapprove of," he said, and he felt the Prince's mind pucker up around his affection for the girl. She had once referred scornfully to love's *angoisse vésperale*, evening distress, but then had softened of a sudden, tears had come into her eyes, she had put her hand over her mouth as if to discourage a disposition to cry. Under her breath she had added. "Mon Dieu! Quel sentiment de déréliction!"

"Well, I suppose it is all fiddlesticks, as you say, but it is an expensive form of folly. She will take to her bed with a high fever and transfer her *angustia* to her medical duties. How to face those huge heaps of dead leaves, the neurotic patients who besiege her?"

They rode on for a while in silence, the Prince cracking his finger joints with an ill-tempered scowl. That brave girl, he was thinking, having to defend herself from the charm and folly of this suave python of a man. It was quite maddening for he loved Affad also as he would have loved his closest friend.

"I hardly dare to confide my distress in you because you react so violently. What would you say, I wonder, if you knew that I had been trying to make her pregnant – to face total and irrevocable disaster, so to speak, which would have united us definitively. Eh?" The elder man jumped at the confidence but did not comment upon it; he just sat looking straight ahead for a long moment before asking, "Does she know yet? For certain?" and Affad took his arm affectionately as he replied, "Unfortunately yes!" Rather surprisingly the Prince turned his birdbright glance upon him and said with unexpected sympathy, "Bad luck! Poor girl! But it would have rendered your decision to leave her even harder, even more cruel. You have behaved like a great coward in all this business, I feel; you have failed on both sides, Eros and Thanatos. Yes, you may well hang your head, my boy. And I suppose you blame love for all this lack of moral fibre?"

"Fiddlesticks!" said Affad in his turn with a blush which showed that he had felt the force of the reproof. His thoughts had come full circle and settled into the deep gloom engendered by his self-reproach and by the knowledge that in the last analysis it was the secret brotherhood which had the ultimate claims upon his life, and that at any moment they could foreclose upon his future. What a curse it was, after all, this love which set friend against friend, lover against loved. The whole circle of his friendships had shifted, been displaced by Constance's choice of him.

He had spent a no less gloomy moment at the bedside of the recumbent Blanford whose friendship he now treasured almost as much as that of the Prince. "It was my fault for letting her see passages from the bloody novel; it made her understand how crucial your beliefs were to your life . . . you hadn't told her, had you? O God, I am so sorry. But from her point of view you are simpiy ill, so to speak; you are suffering from a dangerous form of religious mania which she must be dying to cure in order to keep you!" Affad wrung his hands as he listened. He implored his friend to spare him any further analysis. The "bloody" novel lay before Blanford on the bed. He touched it wistfully from time to time with an air of deep regret. "Sebastian, please forgive me!" he said.

Affad rose. He stood for a while looking down upon the

troubled face of his recumbent friend with affection and sympathy. "Aubrey!" he said aloud and fell silent. Just the word, like a note in music. He did not add a goodbye for it would have seemed out of place – for he was not going anywhere in the profoundest sense. But he did add: "Please write to me when you feel like it; I am not sure when I shall come back, but my intention of the moment is to return in three or four months."

"I know you will come back. I have begun to see a little way into the pattern, the apparent confusion is beginning to make sense. I realise now that I came to Egypt because I was ill, I was afraid of the man on my back. I did a Sinbad in the hope of ridding myself of Sutcliffe – you will have noticed my various attempts to dispense with him, to make him commit suicide for example, using the bridge as a symbol. I had to have my spine shot into holes before I realised that the only way to deal with the Socratic Voice is to concretise it, let it live, manifest itself. Then it becomes a harmless ghost, it passes off in a fever, it writes the classic phrase for you. It can do everything but love. That you must do for yourself."

"O God!" said Affad dismally. "*Again!*"

"I had formed him just as one forms a renal calculus – or a teratoma, or the shadowy figure of one's twin which must be thrown by the ever-present witness of birth, the placenta. To hell with all this verbiage! The creature is alive, he is coming to lunch, he will even get an O.B.E. in a while for his services to the Crown. O God, Sebastian, I wish you were staying; I have learned so much from you!"

Still his friend said nothing but simply stood looking down at him affectionately. Blanford had become very thin and pale and drawn-looking; the spinal operations had taken their toll of his health, but so far they had been successful, and the surgeons believed that the next and most critical would be the last. After that it was up to the musculature to recover its tone once more, and for the patient to begin to dream of sitting up, and then walking once more. It seemed such a dream from this vantage point in time. He himself hardly dared contemplate the thought for fear of an ultimate disappointment. He poured out some mineral water from the bottle at his bedside and drank down a draught, but not without pledging his companion ironically in the harmless brew. Alcohol for the nonce was forbidden or he would have proposed a drink in token of farewell. But it was better thus.

So Affad had taken his leave in a thoughtful and sorrowful silence. And the same afternoon while the nurse was bathing and dressing Blanford, Constance looked in for a brief, unexpected visit – the new Constance, so to speak. For she was pale with sleeplessness and professional stress and her talk was languid and of an unusual vagueness. She did not mention her lover, nor did he, for his own distress and confusion were further deepened by the obstinate knowledge that he himself loved her and regretted the harm caused by his selfishness and self-importance. They sat for a while in silence, her hand lying upon his arm, full of an unstressed affection, and perhaps a tiny bit pleading, as if for sympathy. They were not at the end of their surprises, it would seem. It was the death of Livia, now.

To her immense surprise the information had come as a profound shock to Felix Chatto, of all people – he had been almost physically knocked over by it. All his new social assurance and devil-may-care airs had deserted him. The easy splendour of the man of the world – it had vanished, to leave in its place a frightened undergraduate. It was indeed a profound puzzle to the boy himself – yes, while Livia was alive he had lavished an adolescent attachment upon her; but he had never had any faith in his own feelings, he just enjoyed making his friend Aubrey suffer – as apparently had she. Now with the knowledge that Constance brought him he had made the discovery that, after all, he must have loved her – for he loved her still, retroactively, retrospectively – he was sick with the thought of her disappearance, even though he had hardly spared her a thought in all these long mysterious months during which she had vanished and her continuing existence could only be supposed! (I am sick, thought Constance, of sitting at bedsides and prescribing sedatives!) But this paradoxical behaviour touched and interested her, as much as it seemed to surprise the boy himself. He was, for example, avid for every scrap of information concerning the death of Livia; he wanted to know in great detail how she had been found, how the body had been cut down and disposed of, even such minor points as the slit vein in the thigh – Constance had humoured the old superstition about being buried alive by accident in which her sister had believed, and made sure with a femoral incision! She remembered her own insistence upon every scrap of detail in the case of Sam's death – how she had implored Blanford to tell her everything down to the smallest fact, pain her though it might. It was a way of mastering pain to absorb it like this – she now recognised that Felix Chatto was doing the same thing.

It was curious also that the references to Smirgel, the German informer who had enjoyed a somewhat enigmatic if not mysterious relationship with Livia, touched a chord in the memory of Felix – for he recalled that when they were all together in Provence before the war Livia's disappearances often seemed attributable to the existence of a German scholar who had been entrusted with the task of restoring some of the more famous paintings in the town collection. He was rather older than Livia and seemed a harmless, scholarly personage. Was it Smirgel? And did their attachment date from then? She must ask Affad to find out; then all of a sudden she felt the wild pang of her lover's absence like a knifethrust in the loins.

"It *must* have been him, Smirgel!" she cried with undue emphasis, to stifle the pain of the memory. "He told me he was restoring two famous ones. One was Clement's *Cockayne*."

Where had this memory surfaced from? She did not know. Felix said: "Someone was filling her head with stuff about Goethe and Kleist and Novalis with which she would bore the devil out of poor Aubrey who was reciting Keats in his sleep. Somehow I must get over this soon, I can't let her spoil my life by accident like this." So love had its ignominious side also?

Constance walked back to the clinic in a quiet despair at ever restoring the world around her to some sort of coherence. She told herself: "There's a barrier that goes down between you – the process starts at *first sight*, Shakespeare was perfectly right, like Petrarch, like Marlowe. Click! Of a sudden you are thinking each other's thoughts. Every other mental predisposition seems meaningless, trivial, vulgar. . . . There is nothing more to understand, it would seem!" Clouds had formed and swung low over the lake preparing for one of those electrical thunderstorms which punctuate life in mountain scenery. She was still living out the supreme collision of that first embrace, now so far back in time that it seemed prehistoric. Yet it was there, ever-present on the surface of her thought. She had changed very much. In the margin of a book she had borrowed from Sutcliffe she had found the scribbled words: "The same people are also others without realising it." The wind had risen and the waters of the lake were marked with dark prints of paws. The sky had swelled, as ominous as the nervous breakdown she could feel approaching her across the water. She tried once or twice to weep but it did not work; her mind was as dry as a bone. Then it started raining and she ran the last hundred yards to the ferry with her handbag held above her head.

Schwarz her doctor associate sat like a graven image at his desk reading the *News of the World* raptly. After long days spent with the insane he found these excursions into reality, as he called them, most refreshing; in this long catalogue of crime and folly, of mishaps and maladies, he felt that the real world was asserting itself, marking out its boundaries. It saw precarious, full of penalties – for one slip of the tongue or the mind and one became food for the doctor or the psychiatrist, a tenant of this quiet hotel set among lawns and orchards beside the lake. Here among the worm-casts of old theologies they knew for certain that science had abdicated, that the law of entropy ruled. Reality which was once so very "real" now only manifested a "tendency to exist"! All truth had become provisional and subject to scale. Truth was only true "on the whole". Someone, perhaps Schwarz himself, had scribbled upon the blackboard above her desk the verse:

Though dice thrown twice
May remain the same dice
Yet chancy their fall
For hazard is all!

But when he looked up from his paper and caught sight of his colleague's distraught expression he felt a thrill of sympathetic alarm, for he knew his Constance well and knew the limits of her strength. It was a moment of great stress, of great danger, he could feel it. He folded his paper and drew a deep breath, deciding as he did so to make a lightning decision. He would not indulge the advancing illness by suggestions of rest and careful sedation – he would risk exhausting her further but pushing her onward into a case which might occupy her mind and temper her distress. He said, hardly giving himself time to think the matter out, "Look, Constance, I have come to a decision about Mnemidis, but I want to talk it over with you before acting. I have decided that we should surrender him to the authorities and freely admit that we can do nothing with him. He is too sane or too mad. It's idle to talk of treatment. Besides, I am afraid of him, which is bad in a therapist! I was listening to the transcriptions again last night. It's no good. He is acting all the time, even to himself!"

Constance was already on her feet with her cheeks flushed. "You *can't!*" she cried with a vehemence that did his heart good to hear. "He is the most *interesting* case we have ever had. What a waste to let him rot away in the high security prison for twenty years, without trying to at least document the paranoia. It would be a shame – what on earth are you thinking about?"

"My skin, frankly. He is dangerously sane and altogether too articulate for our safety. I'm lost, Constance. Listen for yourself – everything he says is true and yet it's all false. It all comes to the boil, slowly and then . . . bang! – a crime. From another point of view it's a waste of time, of our time, for there are cases we *can* help. Don't you see?"

"No, I don't! And if you won't continue with him I shall take your place. I'm not afraid of him. Besides, you have the old 'Malabar' at hand if anything goes wrong, gets out of hand. I implore you to reconsider the matter; let me take a hand for a bit with him. He has not discussed the actual murders yet, has he?"

'Not in detail; he is busy trying to justify himself at the moment – and with what ability, it's hair-raising! I am supposed to see him today. I was going to tell him about my decision and pack him off back to prison to complete his sentence."

"Shame!" she said, and taking his hand in her own firm grip went on, "Let me take over the session from you. Besides, I need something to get my teeth into, something to keep my time fully engaged! Mnemidis the impersonator would be just it. Please let me!"

Schwarz made a show of hesitation and indecision. But as a matter of fact he was seriously wondering whether the decision was in fact a wise one; various factors in the case made him wonder whether the arrival of a woman doctor on the scene would not aggravate matters. He hovered between all these contingencies with an exquisite sense of vertigo. By doing this in order to restore the balance he felt was at risk in

Constance he might . . . "O Jesus!" he said, and he was not a pious man, although a Jew, "O Jesus, help!"

In hospital parlance the "Malabar" was just a strong-arm man who was always on hand to deal with dangerous or refractory patients. There were several in the employ of the clinic, but Pierre was their favourite – a giant negro from Martinique who combined overwhelming physical force with a warm gentleness, a ruthlessness of affection that had even the most difficult patients at his mercy in no time. "Pierre is bringing him – indeed, there they are! If you feel you *can*, then perhaps you should, Constance! But I have misgivings. Look at them."

The guard and the patient advanced through the forest side by side at an easy pace. Mnemidis was of a slight build but with very long arms and a strange domed head which gave him a somewhat professorial look – belied by his curious and sordid record. He glanced furtively sideways and upwards at the negro face of his keeper; they could not hear what he was saying but his expression was ingratiating. The negro did not walk, he sailed serenely onwards with eyes half closed – almost, you might have said, a sleep-walker. But he had one hand twisted lightly into the cuff of Mnemidis' coat and with this invisible leverage he was actually propelling him gently in the direction of the psychiatrists' lodge with its array of confessionals. They watched for a moment; then Constance was at the door. "I shall take him today," she said with a new decision, "and give you a rest." But Schwarz called after her: "Maximum security, don't forget, please!" He had not forgotten the episode with the metal paper knife which could have cost him at the least a wound, at the most his life.

But Constance was an experienced practitioner of the black arts, and as she slid into her seat at the bare desk she tested the soft bell which might summon a waiting "Malabar" to her aid, and also checked the hidden Judas through which

Schwarz, if he so wished, might cast an occasional glance into the theatre of operations. A recording apparatus existed though its functioning was often doubtful because of the fixed microphone. A patient lying on the couch was fairly recorded, but if he became agitated and moved about as so often they did, or even simply sat up – as Mnemidis was just about to do – why, the recording was scrambled.

She composed her hands upon the desk before her and waited for the door to open and for Pierre to usher in his charge, which he now did with a kind of dusky dignity which showed kindness and insight – for there is nothing more humiliating than to be shoved around when one is ill and knows it. But then Mnemidis might have phrased it otherwise for he spoke of it as "feeling real", and contrasted it with less heightened states which he called "feeling normally unreal". Quite a card, this man who sidled into the room looking about him as if recognising invisible onlookers who would certainly be amused by his predicament. "And where is Dr Schwarz?" he demanded at once on an insolent note and waited for Constance to explain the substitution. But it would have been an error to do this from a sitting position while he stood over her, and to redress the situation in her favour she said with quiet authority, "You can lie down, please. And put your handbag on the table where we can see it." He did not like this at all and flashed alarmed glances everywhere, but she waited there impassive, staring at him, until slowly he started to consider obeying her. It was important that the female handbag (in cheap crocodile skin) should be deposited between them, for it contained his power, his malefic genius. It was probably quite empty, but for him it was a kind of bomb, at once defensive and aggressive. So long as he put it down somewhere he was disarmed. Well, he put it down, and she sighed with relief.

He lay there for a while, smiling and pouting at old memories, while she watched him thoughtfully and reproached herself for the fact that underneath everything – if sincerity counted for anything – she was disposed towards this audience because she half hoped to hear the name of another Alexandrian, her lover, Affad! Even though she knew that they could never have met or had anything to do with each other! Mnemidis had hardly seen the place since his acting gift took him all round the world. "Where to begin?" he repeated wistfully, under his breath. Then after a long pause he drew a deep breath and began: "The thing is this: how could things have been otherwise? What could I do? Have you ever thought about the predicament of being God for example – suppose one were? You couldn't act otherwise. In my case – ah! listen carefully. In my case I was born without aptitudes or inclinations, and with little enough brains or beauty. I was just *there*, my mind as smooth as an egg, but with no direction, apparently good for nothing, and so society must suffer me. . . . O God, the emptiness, it leads directly to a state of alienation, one feels the fact of being a sort of cosmic mishap! The intense *boredom* is crushing. In my case it led however to a state of grace. By an accident I discovered a *sortie*. An opening. I found that without being actually great you can slip past the sentries into greatness, without waking the sacred geese . . ."

A spasm of violent nausea seized him and he turned up his eyes into his head in a frightening grimace which seemed almost epileptoid. It died down slowly, leaving him pale and weary-looking.

"Well?" she said, in order to keep contact.

"Well!" he echoed. "One night at a party, suddenly and quite involuntarily I uttered a false laugh, in a vague desire to amuse. The cracked hysterical laugh of a servant girl. It had such an instant success that I was as if stamped for life as an impersonator. I became in demand at parties where I would laugh until I had everyone shrieking with mirth, or trembling with anxiety for sometimes it went on too long, I could not break it off." He put his hands to his throat as if exploring old bruises.

"Then gradually the voices came, I developed a whole repertoire, it was like becoming a hotel with someone different in each room. Yes, but you could mix up the keys if you weren't careful. Laughing professionally before a public – that is something different. I began to voyage among the living and the dead – at the suggestion of my lover, an old man weighed down with his culture. Werther, Kleist, Manfred, Byron, Hamlet, he could not divest himself so he voided them all on me. I did not read anything, you understand, but he directed me and coached me and instructed me so they were more real to me than if I had read them myself. Gradually as I improved in richness I added other touches, sudden frightening grimaces, choking and falling, enacting a shooting star or a flash of lightning. A pistol shot, a groan, a sigh – Casimir developed these thoughts and planted them in me so that I enacted them. But now I had entered a new domain of total joylessness. I felt the strain. You see, right from the beginning this man had enslaved me against my own will. It's common enough in Egypt, this sort of magic. When I refused his first advances he used magic. His wife Fatima told me long afterwards how it worked – she too was forced by his threats. He forced her to perform fellatio on him, holding her by the chignon, clamped. With his free hand he dialled my number and engaged in a long amorous pleading conversation – leaving me in no doubt as to what was being done to him and by whom. At the moment when he felt his sperm pass into the mouth of Fatima I felt it also for he had visualised my 'eidolon' as we say. I cried out and dropped the phone, but it was done. Next day I woke with a headache and a fever and a sore throat. I dreamed of him. I was on fire. Finally I was so exhausted by the mental waves he was sending me – the sheer weight – that I capitulated and asked him to come. I could not wait, I was in a frenzy of capitulation.

"So it came about. He was active and vicious but very clever and a magician with money. But his look was so sad and disabused, his eyes so ignorant of smiling, that it gave one a thrill: one was talking to a dead man, one felt. He used to say, 'Time is rusting away inside me, my heart is full of barbed wire.' I no longer hated him, the hate had dulled. I was his slave and I hated only myself. Yet he must *pay* one day, I felt it. I was not surprised when the stranger came from the city with a message. A new era had already begun. The veins in my head had started to swell with water, throbbing: echoing: booming! It was this stranger who asked me if it wasn't right that Casimir should *pay*, should die. There was no other real solution, it would seem; the little group of his friends had turned against him. They were looking for a passive instrument – that is how he put it. Passive. Instrument. I watched him curiously when he was asleep, he seemed so near to death already. Once he felt my gaze on him and he opened one eye and said: 'You know this is with my *full* consent? Don't be afraid to act if they ask!' Could it be possible that he knew?

"I had started my tricks already – I was imitating his voice on the telephone and ordering things from shops, all in his name. A mountain of jewellery was what I felt I needed to counter my ugliness. He knew but said nothing. As for Fatima, I left her for another occasion, another country, another method. The symptoms were much the same but the powder left no trace in the organs though she had already denounced me by letter, for she had been warned."

Constance listened with intense concentration to this professional monologue, to this desolate man, empty of all feeling. He went on: "I discovered that even when I was *acting*, I myself was only acting. Where had I gone? My I? My eye?"

The desolation of the liar! He was nodding slowly with the mandarin-like nodding of the morphinomane – though he was not one in real fact. He was only illustrating time running on, running out. "Tick-tock," he said. "So it goes on. Tick-tock. Do you carry a watch, like all doctors do? May I see it, please?" As a matter of fact she did, in the fob-pocket of her white smock. It was a pretty little timepiece, slightly ovoid, almost egg-shaped. She placed it on the table before him and he took it up with a sort of shy rapture, examining it with close attention, holding it to his ear. Then he swallowed it right before her very eyes and they gazed at each other with silent amazement, for he himself seemed astonished by his own action. It was important not to over-react, as with a child who swallows a peach-stone. She stared. "Why," she said at last, "did you do that?" and he shook his head with a childish expression of wonder on his face: "I don't know. I suddenly needed to stop the world. It was stronger than me. I stopped *his*, didn't I? In spite of our romance I stopped it thoroughly, once and for all. But this wasn't very clever of me, I admit."

The hour was up according to the electric clock on the wall and she rose. "I will tell Pierre," she said. "He will know what to do."

"I don't feel like apologising," he said and his underlip trembled as if he was about to start crying. She pressed the bell and the vast form of the negro appeared in the doorway, smiling. She explained what had happened in the most matter of fact way and seemed by her tone to reassure the sick man for he smiled and nodded. Pierre took his sleeve with a tactful nonchalance and they set off back to the dangerous ward together, walking away circumspectly through the trees. She watched them disappear and then slipped back to her own room, only to find that Schwarz had also gone. A passage from his new book was on the typewriter and she bent down to read it. "But Freud like Darwin was truthful to the point of holiness. Their devout scientific atheism had the necessary rigour to produce results. When you look through a telescope of high magnification you must hold your breath so the image does not waver. Now, how poor the dialogue has become. Not science but semantics rules! Paris, instead of playing a seminal role to replace the murdered Vienna has reaffirmed its lesser role as the capital of fashion in ideas, of superficiality. Spindrift of politics fabricated by educated poltroons with taste. *Barbe à papa*, a candy-floss culture."

Schwarz had grown increasingly critical of the French rôle during the war. "As Darwin himself noted: 'To reason while observing is fatal – but how useful afterwards!'" While she read, her colleague himself appeared, with his mildly sardonic air of curiosity and amusement. "Well?" he said, and she gave an account of her session with Mnemidis and his gesture with her watch. He laughed with delight and said: "Poor Pierre will have to spend his days stool-watching until it reappears, if it ever does. How do you know – he may digest it! Thank God, however, for the session seems to have done *you* some good!" As they talked he had placed his fingers upon her pulse. "And your colour is good once more!" Perhaps the demon of this fatigue would pass and her composure be restored by itself? "I have had another insulting letter from Sutcliffe, probably written when he was drunk." He took up a sheet of official notepaper and read out slowly, "'Schwarz, you bloody man, supporter of lost causes among which Love looms largest, why not try another method? Instead of fretting about *changing* the world, why not realise and accept it as it is, admitting that its order is divine, that reality, of which we are part, realises itself *thus*. Swallow the whole thing whole! If you did, if you do, the great paradox will supervene; the world will automatically and irremediably change itself and of its own accord. Or so they say! Farewell!'"

"He has been drinking again I don't doubt. I think you must really join him one day for a game of billiards."

Schwarz looked startled. "Blood sports! Me?" He made defensive gestures with his hands. They were finished for the day and uncertain of how to fill up the evening. He thought he would probably go to the cinema, while she thought with dread of her empty flat. It seemed more than ever desirable to unearth some company which might help her to pass the remaining daylight hours without too much room for introspection! Schwarz seemed equally solicitous about her balance. He said, "Constance, when are you going to see the small boy of Affad – the autistic one?" She sat down and reflected. "I don't know. I am in such a disturbed state at the moment that I thought to let things settle down a bit."

Schwarz shook his head. "I should start at once," he said, "at least to make the opening moves. After all, there may be nothing to be done. The children of the rich and purseproud are always in the greatest danger."

Children!

She remembered Affad declaiming in a mocking voice something like: "Children! you were born to disappoint your parents as we have all been, for our parents built us gilded and padded cages to live happily-ever-after-in – and look what came about: exile, bereavement, folly, voyages, despair, ecstasy, illness, love, death: all life in a single stab like a harlot's kiss."

She was thinking sadly of the absent Affad and suddenly coming to herself she saw that Schwarz was contemplating her with solicitude and concern, trying to estimate just where she stood in the face of this crisis in her affairs. "My God! what a shabby profession it is – or perhaps it is us, worn out by the sheer magnitude of the task and the limitations imposed by inadequate knowledge. I have started dishing out pills, the first sign of morbid frustration. And our job is to teach our clients how to rediscover a state of joyful nonchalance in the face of things, something as calm as death but just *not* death . . . And here we are falling sick ourselves. I'm worried about you. You have become a bore." Thus Schwarz.

"You mean in love! I know it!"

"But that is not why he left?"

"No. It's more complicated."

It was both more complicated and yet quite simple, quite transparent. "You know what I think? I think I will try to patch up my wounded self-esteem by buying that fur coat which I need for the winter. I have been putting it off all the year. It seems just the moment. Do you think it will save the day?"

"Yes. The instinct is sound!" he said, not without a tinge of irony. He was about to add that it was one of Lily's habits when she felt depressed, but was suddenly assailed by a pang of depression at the thought of her, at the thought of having betrayed her, as he put it to himself. When going to the cinema he tried to avoid the newsreels which preceded the big film, lest they show scenes of the advances into Germany. "And those pictures," she said, "that's another reason – I found them on Affad's desk, the whole exhibition folio spread out on the floor. They are mind-blenching in their horror. It's quite beyond weeping. One wanted to bang one's head on the wall from sheer incomprehension. How *could* they? How *could* we?"

Schwarz sighed and drew obscure diagrams on the writing pad at his elbow.

The confusions caused by the onset of war had been great, but had given place to a certain artificial order during the prosecution of it over a period of years. Some sort of haphazard system had emerged based on the prevailing military and political options. Now with the return of a hesitant and fragmentary quasi-peace this factitious order was once more disturbed and on an even wider scale, for the whole world by now had reeled out of orbit under the hammer blows of the sick Germany. The confusions engendered by this peace were almost worse; Switzerland was an oasis of calm, an island, compared to the surrounding hinterland which was so fully occupied with the disbanding of armies, resettlement of disturbed populations, onerous shortages, dislocated communications, broken civic threads everywhere which must be retied, respooled. The terrifying photographs of which she spoke had been taken by the armies as they advanced, and they were of concentration camps and their inmates. Everyone had known about the extermination camps, it is true, but people find things hard to realise, to accept what they might intellectually know. The Red Cross had received all this frightful documentary material with instructions from the military and political arm to give it the widest possible publicity; and to this end the pictures had been enlarged and an exhibition formed which showed the work of the camps in all their dreary horror. The idea was to mount a travelling public exhibition together with an illustrative text in several languages. Blanford had been approached for that and the whole project had been the subject of a number of committee meetings.

"I was intrigued to see from the minutes," said Constance, "that you came out rather strongly *against* the display idea for the pictures. We thought that as a Jew the subject . . ."

Schwarz made a noise like a snort and said, "*Aber*, Constance, I am first of all a doctor, and my decision was according. The subject is horrible, the injustice and horror palpable, but on such a scale should we turn it into a peepshow? Of course the thing must stay on the record and we will somehow have to try and forgive what it will be impossible to forget. But finally this whole-scale outbreak of German *lustmorder* was a national aberration on a fantastic scale. What is even more interesting though is that they managed to start the French off behaving like that at first; doubtless the British would have followed suit if the Channel expedition had come off. All this raises a medical and philosophic problem of such great importance that we must try and study it coolly, as we are trying to study Mnemidis. What a triumph it would be if we could throw that Faustian switch and get him working with rather than against us. Roughly, all that was in my mind when I voted against."

"I see."

"I wonder if you do. I know that Affad does because I was able to discuss it with him, and of course in the new book I try and deal with the whole matter in general terms. Our whole civilisation is enacting the fall of Lucifer, of Icarus!"

She felt a rush of affection for all that he had given her over the years and a quickening of love and admiration for the dignity of the man and his faithfulness to his craft. He worshipped method like the wise old god he was. "Affad was right when he said that the most tragic thing about the German decision to abolish the Jews was that their solution, for all the horrible pain and suffering it brought, was profoundly *frivolous* – cruel paradox! For the problem of the Jews is far more serious, not less, concerning as it does an alchemical *prise de position* on the vexed question of matter. Demos Demos Democritos . . . now we see that matter is not excrement but thought. If we have come to the end of this cycle and are now plunging into a hubristic *dénouement* I can't help as a Jew being deeply proud of the tremendous intellectual achievement of Jewish thought. I am thinking of our three great poets of matter. What a stupendous Luciferian leap into the darkness of determinism. Will there be time to correct the angle of vision, that's what worries and intrigues me? This Jewish passion for absolutism and matter has already started to modify itself – entropy is the new sigil! Freud arrived on the scene like a new Merlin to take up the challenge of the Delphic oracle. He resolved the riddle of Oedipus. A Hero! He paid for it with his organ of speech, just as Homer and Milton each paid for his inner vision with his sight! But the confusion of gold and matter is a philosophic problem, and you can't deal with it by abolishing the Jews' physical presence. Our racial passion must become less visceral and more disinterested. The Jewish mind cannot *play* as yet! O Christ, what does all this rigmarole matter? Who will read my book? They will say that I am anti-Jewish!"

"Yes," she said. "I am familiar with this line of thought because of . . ." – strange that she should have a kind of inhibition about pronouncing his name – "Affad!" There! but it made her feel shy. "Unhappily we still have a need for heroes. Myths cannot get incarnated and realised fully in the popular soul which seeks this nourishment with sacrifices, for reality is just not bearable in its banal daily form, and the human being, however dumb he is, is conscious of the fraud."

"Yes. It's what that bastard Jung is up to. Affad approves a little bit but not entirely of his attitude. The alchemical work is in distillation or decoction – the personal ego decants itself in thoughts which are really acts and slowly, drop by amazing drop, virtue, which is voidness, precipitates." They both laughed, he with that sardonic helpless Viennese despair which had taken so many generations to form. It was not cynicism. It was a profound creative distrust of the dispositions taken up by reality, by history. He said softly, "A sort of *pourriture de soi* . . ."

They were both wondering what Mnemidis would have made of this conversation – highly articulate as he was. How could one talk to him about such matters, which were after all vital for his health, his recovery? His response would be "acted": for him all love was the genius of misgiving, which rules the human heart.

Schwarz was sick to death of this world and its works. Even as he felt the pulse of Constance under his fingers he felt rise in his own soul the thick sediment of despair, like the lees of a bad wine, which dragged him always towards suicide – the suicide which always seemed to him so inevitable. One day it would claim him, of that he was sure. At such moments when the demon had him by the hair he wanted to bury his face between the breasts of a woman and hide from this all-pervading idea.

"I dreamed last night that we killed Mnemidis with one simple injection; you helped me. We were so happy to be delivered from him!" He sighed and cleaned his old horn-rimmed glasses and he thought to himself, "It's a question of patience. The vast weight of cosmic submission, the inertia of mass, will prevail over all."

"I'd like a dry Martini," she said.

"Done!" he said, stripping off his white tunic.

They took the ferry across the lake whose glassy surface reflected the coming night, and made their way with slow steps across the town – carefully avoiding the old Bar de la Navigation, for they did not want any more talk – and slowly arriving at the main station of the town where they sought out the first-class buffet, incomparable for the size and quality of its pre-war Martinis. The barman was an old friend, and had in his youth worked at the Ritz in Paris. Yes, they wanted to sit quite quiet in a companionable silence. And this came about as planned except that as they sat down he said, "I am profoundly worried about you." And she replied, "I know you are – I have a juicy neurasthenia coming on, like influenza. It will pass, you will see." No more. Just that and the alcohol burning in the mind like a spirit lamp. And of course, dimmed by the heavy doors, all the distant romantic stirring of trains arriving and departing.

Recently, within the last three months, she had had an accidental meeting with someone which she would soon come to regard increasingly as providential; it surprised her that she had not mentioned it to him, since it had involved her in an entirely new programme of personal health, personal endeavour: moreover in a field which she had long regarded as suspect and without much interest for a scientist. Walking one day along the old rue de la Conféderation with Felix Chatto, en route for a coffee-shop where they could gossip, they came face to face with a small white-clad figure which at first neither could recognise. It at first looked like an Indian saint, a yogi of some sort. Its mane of white hair flowed down on either side of its dark negroid features. It was clad in white in the manner of an Indian *sadu* or holy man, and it was walking barefoot on the grubby pavements. This was the figure that spread its arms in a signal of surprised recognition and stood stock still, smiling at them. Who on earth could it be? They peered at the apparition, peered through the tangle of silver hair, as one might peer into the jungle, intent on the identification of some strange animal. The little sage had the advantage of them for he said, "My goodness, Mr Chatto, sir, and Miss Constance, fancy meeting you! What are you doing here?"

What were they doing there! And slowly piercing the obscurity of the Indian saint's disguise they gradually found with the help of memory another face emerge, developed like a photograph. "Max!" she cried, and with a short interval of prolonged puzzlement Felix Chatto echoed her with "Max!" Then they were all three shaking hands, embracing, talking at once. It was the old valet-chauffeur of Lord Galen, whom they had last seen during the last summer they had all spent together in Provence; the old negro boxer who used to be Lord Galen's humble sparring partner on the lawn at daybreak! How was it that he had so completely vanished from their thoughts – the violet chauffeur who often dressed like an Italian admiral? "Max!" she said, "You have changed so much – what has happened?" And in his affectionate excitement he almost reverted to his old Brooklyn-negroid tones. "Doogone it, Miss Constance, everything! Just everything! Ah been in India a while now and ah've learned a new science. Better than the old one-two!" He spread his arms and his face took on an angelic expression of bliss and devoutness. They both felt suddenly abashed by Max in this new incarnation, this new disguise – if disguise it was. Still holding their hands in his he explained breathlessly how the transformation had come about. "When Lord Galen went home I decided to go to India. I had received several invitations from an old man who made a lot of sense to me – I met him in Avignon. He came to the boxing booth where I used to drop in for a work-out. But he wasn't a boxer, he was a wrestler and a yoga-maker. I got to working with him a little, and was intrigued enough to visit him in Bombay. Thanks to him I became a yoga-maker and teacher; when I was through he asked me to run one of his groups right here in Geneva. So here I am!"

It seemed almost unbelievable; such a transformation of personality in such a short space of time, it seemed almost like witchcraft. They dragged him off to a coffee-shop where they sat him down before a dish of tea and cakes in order to ply him with questions about this new departure. The only one of them who had shown any interest in yoga as a method of health regeneration had been Livia; but perhaps this fact had not been known to Max at that far-off epoch – indeed her own initiation into the science had come about in Germany during her flirtation with National Socialism. But Constance did not mention her name – why should she? The gravity and simplicity with which Max talked about the change of mind involved in developing from a pugilist into a yogi was more than merely interesting – she was struck by the distinctions he drew and the simple vividness with which he enunciated them. How he had changed! India had even improved his English, as well as giving him at times a tiny touch of a Bengali accent. Constance was beside herself with joy, and when Felix Chatto was forced to take himself off to the office she had stayed on for a full hour, profoundly interested in the psychological change which had taken place in this old friend. "Of course our studio yoga isn't a therapy as such but since I have been here I've seen such dramatic changes in people due to its practice that I have begun to wonder jest what in hell it is. Now doctors are sending people to us that they can't handle. Our classes are full of young people suffering from stress and tension of spirit – on their way to crack-ups we help them to avoid. In India they'd be surprised, since there's no ego to get mentally stressed up with, so to speak. But why don't you come and see the studio? My, it's classy, it's downright classy. And I'm the boss locally – crazy, isn't it?"

Later that evening she actually did visit it with him and watched a hatha class under the instruction of a young girl. It created a sort of echo in her, a half-formulated desire to become part of it, to learn the ritual. After all, what was her medical practice about if it was not concerned with the problems of stress in its extreme forms? Why should she not study this ancient method for a while and see what bearing it had upon her own formulations?

Later still, sitting in his tiny office drinking more tea, it seemed to her the most natural thing in the world for him to lean forward and touch her knee as he said, "You know, I believe you could work with us and learn something you could turn to use. Maybe, if you had the patience . . ."

She smiled and replied, "I've always had the patience to learn something new; but tell me how and where to begin." And the negro smiled and went on patting her hand as he said, "If you like I'll step out with you to the ten cent store where you can buy yourself a cheap yoga mat. It's the first really important act, for you will find it very important for you; you'll get sort of stuck on it. It's like all your work and your breathing, and your whole mentality soaked into it while you work on it, or maybe just lie on it and rest. They don't cost much, they are just little eiderdowns as you saw in class. But it's good to get a colour you like and keep it always around you – you'll want to anyway. The thing becomes precious, like your own hymn book. It's a record of your strivings." He went on in this vein while conducting her downstairs and across the inner courtyard to the front entrance on the street. They ambled across to a store and she duly bought herself the small eiderdown as required. Then she accompanied him back for her first lesson. The studio was indeed rather a grandiose modern establishment forming part of a flourishing Turkish bath. When they re-entered the main courtyard she was struck by the singular vision of two yoga students diligently burning up their eiderdowns on a lighted brazier. Astonished by this aberrant conduct she stopped and pointed it out to Max. "What on earth . . . ?" she cried, nonplussed. He burst out laughing: "They've *realised!*" he said cryptically.

She was completely nonplussed. "But after what you have just been saying about yoga mats . . ." she said in bewilderment, but he only shook his head and laughed at greater length. "Listen," he said at last, "there is nothing mysterious about what they are doing, but I don't want to go into merely intellectual explanations. It's better left – the subject for the time being. Later on you'll get it for yourself."

They resumed their trudge up the stairs and then, as she debated, a sudden intuition flashed upon the screen of her thoughts. She stopped dead and said, "I think I have got it! Attachment!"

"Yeah," he said with a grin. "That's it!"

She surprised herself by this sudden and quite spontaneous formulation. Where had it come from? Obviously she must have read it somewhere – for after all the whole subject of Eastern metaphysics was quite foreign to her study and indeed her interest. "You know more than you realise," he said happily. "Now I'm putting you in the beginners class so you can jest learn the alphabet; later on the letters will make words and then the words will make sentences – that is if you don't get bored and jest drop the whole thing. It does happen and it isn't important. The science is for those who reely want it and need it and are prepared to make an effort. Like me wanting to become a *champ* – it was an obsession, and I made sacrifices to get there. However it didn't work, I didn't have the class. Then age took a hand and I lost out."

"And now?" she asked.

"Bless you, I'm jest happy without any kind of after-thoughts. They showed me how one could meditate sweetly and gradually harmonise with the goings-on of the whole wide world!"

"It sounds great!"

"It certainly is. I'm telling *you!*"

And so had begun her insinuation into the mysteries of the craft, and now while she thought back upon it she realised why she had never mentioned it to her colleague. He had once or twice hinted that all such matters whose provenance was Indian were somewhat intellectually disreputable in a scientist of the twentieth century: and she valued his good opinion! If ever asked she had been wont to say that twice a week she took a relaxing Turkish bath in the town. So the yoga had remained a secret between herself and Max. Yet not completely – for later Affad had redeemed this whole field of knowledge by admitting something that neither Max nor Schwarz could have admitted – namely that the heart of all these dissimilar sciences was the same heart. Max knew no science and Schwarz no yogic lore; she felt herself to be intellectually living in a double life between them, each with his claims upon her time and intelligence. If driven to it Schwarz would even quote Kipling on the question of East being East, etc. But thank goodness one day Affad took up the discussion and surprised her by saying quite simply that "Einstein's non-discrete field, Groddeck's 'It', and Pursewarden's 'heraldic universe' were all one and the same concept and would easily answer to the formulations of Patanjali." Her heart leaped with joy to hear this, for the whole weight of such tiring speculations had been pressing upon her mind, causing her anxiety and muddle in her thoughts, not to mention doubts about her methods. Of course! And one more reason to love Affad – insight was so much more important than physical beauty. As they sat confronting one another in silence she had the sudden physical feeling of his presence beside her – perhaps at that moment he was thinking of her, desiring her. Trains came and went and the forest of human feet pounded the dark pavements of the quais outside the bar. She drank and listened to her own thoughts as they scurried hither and thither like mice: all thoughts of the past. It was strange how this breach in their relationship had stopped her in her tracks – she felt quite futureless, everything lay in the past and was bathed in the sunshine of reminiscence. O where was Affad now?

TWO

The Inquisition

WHERE INDEED? THEIR PLANE WAS DELAYED IN TURKEY by bad weather – the Prince behaved as if it had happened deliberately in order to annoy him further. Nothing would convince him that the Turks ("they have souls of mud like the Nubians") had not organised the whole thing from the depths of their anti-Egyptian feeling, even the weather which was so inclement. They spent a sombre weekend watching rain and cloud lying like smoke upon the echoing vistas of the capital – at its best a proud and sinister place. Even the beauties of the Bosphorus were dazzled and rubbed out by the wind and waves, and a racing darkness. The pleasant excursion to Eyoub which they always took was hardly tempting in such frowning weather. Moreover the subject of the journey and that of Constance weighed heavily between them; indeed every time these subjects were touched upon the Prince flew into a vehemence and was so acid that the long-suffering Affad began to wax irritated. They sat among palms in the hotel, where the Prince impatiently read out-of-date newspapers and cracked his finger-joints while Affad played solitaire on a green card table in a self-commiserating sort of manner, swearing from time to time, under his breath and in several languages. The coming Inquisition filled him with guilty gloom and apprehension.

After one sally by the Prince he turned on him and said, "I implore you to drop the subject – I know your views on it too well! I know that I have to face the enquiry and answer for a gross and lamentable failure of nerve – but let me prepare myself quietly for it and not be chivvied out of my mind . . ."

"Who is chivvying *who*?" growled the scowling Prince,

and Affad replied just as testily, "You are. And if you don't stop I'll take another plane."

The Prince snorted with contempt. "*What* other plane I'd like to know!"

It was very much to the point. They had sent a telegram announcing their tardy arrival in Alexandria. The Prince after a moment of silence could not resist a resumption of hostilities. "I hope you'll have the grace to confess that you have exercised a baleful influence on the poor girl – among other things encouraging all this yogi-bogey stuff she has got interested in."

"It's something you would do well to get interested in yourself before you fall apart, Prince. Those awful attacks of sciatica, for example. You could dispense with all those injections. And then your belly . . ."

"What's wrong with my belly?" said the Prince haughtily, mounting his high horse.

"The Princess thinks it too protuberant."

The little man snorted. "People of my rank cannot be expected to stand about in artificial postures dressed in a loin cloth, nor live on goat's milk. Who the hell do you think I am, Gandhi? And all this physical stuff, in my walk of life and at my age . . . it's preposterous. You have influenced a serious scientist with all this Indian mumbo-jumbo. And you, with a degree in economics and humanities!"

It was Affad's turn to pass into a vehemence. He drew a breath and said, "It is quite gratuitous and you are behaving like a Philistine, which you are not. I have already explained to you exactly what yoga is about in scientific terms. There is *nothing* in it that contradicts western science at any point. It is simply spine-culture intended to restore the original suppleness of the muscle schemes of the body and to feed them on oxygen with the help of the lungs. You treat the whole body as a keyboard and muscle by muscle get it back into optimum condition, as supple as a snake or a cat, ideally. The *asanas* are breathing codes. They teach the muscles their role and finally the movements become sort of mental acts. The muscles are oxygen-filled and get to become almost mental acts when they move."

"Rigmarole!" said the Prince firmly. "Mere rigmarole!"

Affad produced a characteristic grunt of indignation. After all, he had not known in any detail the extent of Constance's preoccupation with these new lessons she had started taking – nor indeed did it much concern him, except that they were valuable: for he himself had followed courses in the science long ago and had profited from them. He had in fact cured a recurrent spinal complaint in a period of two years of methodical practice. "Mental acts!" he went on heatedly. "And once informed the muscle stays in trim eternally, or until decrepitude sets in, or illness. I fully approve of her investigations, for that is what they are. And philosophically speaking the whole process is one of progressive cosmic helplessness. It relinquishes its resistance to entropy, and the basic realisation which meditation brings is really n-dimensional. *You* could do with a bit of that yourself. After all your own sexual follies foisted on you by that *idiot* house-doctor of yours! Involving children and dogs and so on, just because you began to fear impotence and were scared to talk to the Princess about it."

This was beginning to be extremely unfair, and the Prince clenched his fists for all the world as if he were about to punch Affad in the eye. He inflated his lungs fully, as if about to launch into a tirade or utter a shout, but he did neither; he remained poised, as it were, for a long moment, and then burst into a prolonged chuckle. "You brute!" he said, and aimed a make-believe blow at Affad's abdomen. "What an unfair thing to say!" Affad shook his head: "*Au contraire*, a moment of yoga would have set your doubts at rest in the matter and avoided all sorts of compromising and ridiculous situations – for a man of your rank, I mean, since you keep bringing it up!"

The Prince reflected deeply, nodding as he thought. "It was a terrible period," he admitted, thinking back no doubt to the brothel in Avignon where he had once organised what he was wont to describe as a "little spree". The thought gave him cold shudders now. Thank goodness he had confided everything in the Princess and with her help recovered his balance, as well (to his surprised relief) as his virility. Now when he thought back upon that period he had cold shudders, for it was clear that if the Princess had left him it would have been not because of his sexual misdemeanours so much as his lack of confidence in her as a confidante. She was keen on her role as wife and helpmeet. He sighed. "Thank God all that is over." And now all of a sudden his evil humour deserted him and was replaced by an affectionate concern for his friend and for the reception he must get from the small committee in Alexandria who awaited the sinner's return. The executive arm of the fellowship was limited to three members who operated with a formal anonymity on behalf of the whole group; but as they were rotated with great regularity every year it was not possible to guess in detail at their composition. Thus the Prince, who would have loved to try and intervene on his friend's behalf, or to use his influence to secure some sort of favourable view of his crime – the word is not too strong – was checked by the fact that he did not know whether he had a personal friend among the three to whom he might appeal. . . . The very idea was of course immoral and unthinkable in the gnostic context, but then it was not for nothing that the Prince was a man of the Orient and impregnated with its labyrinthine strategics!

The night drew on and the thunder rumbled. Affad relinquished his solitaire for some sleepy general conversation before suggesting that they should go to bed and not wait for a summons from the airport which would never come because of the wind and pelting rain.

They shambled up to bed like sleepy bears, and were

woken at three o'clock with the intelligence that the plane was ready to leave within the hour, and would touch down at Alexandria – an unusual concession to the Prince's eminence and also to his wire-pulling which was, as always, inspired.

They dozed for the most part in the ill-lit plane and made their way slowly across the waters, tossing and swaying into Egypt where the inadequate aerodrome had been alerted to light them in along a flare path manifestly too short for any but small wartime planes. A bumping and grinding landing rounded off this disagreeable journey; a chalky greasy dawn was coming up as the office car rounded the last headland by the dunes and entered the sleeping town with its soft whirling klaxon pleading with strings of early camels plodding to market with vegetables. "I shall say no more – except tell me as soon as you can what they say," said the Prince and his companion nodded, smiling wanly. "It's impossible to foresee their judgement," he said, "because it has never happened before, an apostasy like mine. O Lord! It will have created a precedent." He sounded close to tears of misery, which indeed he was. The Prince left him – a dozen servants had been waiting all night on the steps of the town house, wet and miserable but faithful as dogs. They whipped open the door and conjured away his baggage. Affad was driven on; his more modest house was set in a grove of palm trees, back from the boulevard. His garden ran beside that of the museum, and indeed from his cellar there was a secret entrance into its basement. Sometimes after dinner he took his guests through the secret door and into the gloomy crypt where so many treasures (which could not be shown for lack of space) stood or lay, shrouded in sheets. Indeed the museum itself was most charming by yellow candle-light, and he used to carry a branch of Venetian candles with him on such occasions. But his own house was more modestly staffed than that of the Prince; a cook and a butler, the faithful and negligent Said, made up the whole staff.

As his key clicked in the door his valet Said rose from the armchair in which he had spent the night's vigil and advanced, rubbing his eyes but smiling delightedly to see his master again. Affad greeted him affectionately and stood steadily divesting himself until the servant carried away his coats and freed him to advance and make a loving tour of the home in which he had spent so many years of his life – many of them quite alone except for the servants. A clock gave off a soft musical chime as if to welcome him back. The statue of Pallas and the stuffed raven were still on the ledge above the fanlight. His books were arrayed on either side of the Adam fireplace – a fine array of friends. He advanced, touched the covers with his fingers as if to identify and greet the author of each, and then progressed towards the group of Tanagra figures in their glass case. He licked his finger and touched the glass to verify if Said had cleaned in his absence or not. But in reality he was searching for something. The servant came back with his mail – a meagre collection of bills for water and electricity, and appeals for hospitals and homes. No, it was not that. He knew that they must have summoned him to a rendezvous. Normally such a missive would have been slipped under the door. He questioned the servant, but no, he had seen nothing like that. He sat down for a moment and drank the coffee which had been prepared for him as he reflected. Finally in some perplexity – for he had expected an instant and peremptory message – he took himself off to his sumptuous bathroom for a bath and a complete change of clothing, not without a certain feeling of relief. Perhaps the whole business might be delayed for a while? On the other hand, he longed to have it over and done with as summarily as possible.

The weather had changed, it had become suddenly sunny and clear, though the cold sea wind persisted. He dressed carefully and taking a light overcoat walked slowly down the boulevard to the Mohammed Ali Club, greeted here and there by a friend or acquaintance who was pleased to see him back, resuming his Alexandrian life once more. It was on the notice board of the club that he found the missive he had been expecting, addressed to him in a hand he did not know and on a paper without letterhead. It said succinctly, "You will attend an exceptional meeting of the central committee at midnight tonight in the burial theatre of the museum crypt." Only that.

He knew what they must mean by the phrase "burial theatre"; it was the furthest part of the museum crypt and had been at some time part of a necropolis. But successive generations had altered it according to more recent motives until it clearly had served several purposes, with its small arch and portion of nave, and its little amphitheatre. It was a mixture of chapel, Greek theatre, and lecture hall admirably suited to the meetings of their society with its need for lectures or discussions of procedure or indeed prayer-meetings and the reading of minutes. It was called "The Crusaders' Chapel" and "The Coptic Shrine". In its further depths it contained some sculptured aeroliths and some drums of stone purporting to be Babylonian sculpture – a sort of map and calendar of the world supported by the coils of a huge serpent. How well he knew the place! It was here that new members were sworn in and their first act of submission heard. And how very appropriate that it should be an amalgam of so many different things, so suitable to a city which had made a cult of syncretism! It was here that he must answer for his defection. He must attend, then, in due form and order, to hear their reproaches and accept whatever punishment or obloquy was his due. He had not a leg to stand on. He wondered what sort of punishment could be envisaged for such a case.

Preoccupied by these grave deliberations and wounded by a sense of guilt, he ate a solitary lunch at the Union Club, where he found himself agreeably alone in the gaunt dining room. But appetite he had none. Then he walked back to his house and took a siesta – fell into a profound sleep which took in at one span all the various fatigues of the journey. Indeed it was already dark when he awoke with a start, summoned by the little alarm clock by his bed. There was time in hand – too much of it. He had begun to feel impatient. Some invisible hand (for there was no trace of Said) had prepared him a light supper such as he was in the habit of ordering when theatre-going kept him out late. He hardly touched it, but he drank a glass of champagne. It was mildly stimulating, mildly encouraging. Then he hunted for the black carnival domino, supposing that it was the appropriate thing for a penitent to wear. Indeed if the society had any formal uniform it was that, though it was worn as informally and carelessly as the fur tippet and cape of a master of arts. Nevertheless carnival time was their most important yearly meeting with its significant – *carni vale* – farewell to the flesh, as suitable for their Manichean creed as for the Christian.

Punctually at five minutes before the hour he visited the lavatory through the window of which he could study the profile of the museum which at this hour was normally deserted. Yes, there were lights on the staircase, so the three Inquisitors must have made their way in to wait for him down below. For his part he preferred his own private entry. He slipped downstairs and through the kitchen into the cavernous pantry where the private door answered noiselessly to his yale key. He had a pocket torch to light his path as he stepped into the gloom of the crypt. With beating heart he traversed the first cell, a sort of antechamber, and then the second, from which he could see a distant light and hear voices. Was he too soon?

No. The door to the theatre had been blocked by a drum of carved stone and when he arrived there a voice from within called his name and asked if it was indeed he, to which he replied in the required language, "None other". He rolled aside the stone and entered the theatre where they waited for him. He was to sit in the centre, he saw, under a floodlight of great theatrical force, while the three Inquisitors occupied three adjacent stone seats in the main hall, the main theatre. The lighting allowed them or perhaps devised by them was so arranged that all he could see was their hands upon the stone dais before them. They were but vague shapes, and with even vaguer voices. He strained at first to see if by chance one of them might be an acquaintance or personal friend. In vain.

So he entered circumspectly, rolling aside the stone drum, and bowing to the three pairs of white hands sat down and bent his head forward upon his breast in a formally penitential gesture of respect: not for the rank of the Inquisitors for they had no formal rank, having been elected by lottery, but for the organisation they represented with its beehive-like grouping of cells.

A voice intoned, "Sebastian, Thoma, Ptah, Affad Effendi?" and he replied in a whisper, "None other". And he felt himself reverting to his Alexandrian self, his Egyptian self. Each name was like the unfolding of a mummy-wrapping, in a way unbandaging his youth with all its fragility. He felt rise in him, like nausea, the long years of solitude and philosophic speculation which had gone to form the person that he now was, and an involuntary sob rose in his throat. He peered into the dark shapes of his three invigilators but could not discern anything except the vague outline of their heads. Only their ghoulish white hands lay before them on the stone tables which were bare save for a small Egyptian knife with its point turned towards him. Yet the voices, whether they addressed him or spoke together, were matter of fact. He studied the spatulate hands of the one who had spoken his name and felt the vague stirrings of familiarity. Could it be Faraj? Neguid? Perhaps Capodistria? Or Banubula? Impossible to be sure. He gave up.

"Do you know why you are here?"

"Yes."

"Tell us why."

Overwhelmed by the gravity of his fault as only a philosopher could be, Affad answered with a sob in his tone, "To answer for my sudden defection. To be punished, admonished, expelled, executed – whatever you may decide is suitable for this unheard of act of treachery. Even now I find it inexplicable to myself. I fell in *love*." The word fell like a slab of stone closing upon a tomb.

One of the Inquisitors drew in his breath with a sharp hiss, but Affad could not tell which one it was, nor why. He fell on his knees and stretching out his hand like a beggar soliciting alms said, "It seemed to me then that there are spirits of love sent into the world who, if recognised, cannot be resisted, *should* not be resisted at the risk of betraying nature herself. I found myself in this impasse. Hence my apostasy, which I have now fully revoked and abandoned."

There was a long silence. Then the first pair of hands to have spoken clasped themselves and the voice belonging to them continued to speak but in an unhurried and sorrowful manner. "You do not know all," it said. "But you know full well that the strength of a chain is the strength of its weakest link. You were prepared to snap the chain of our corporate activities, to prejudice the whole spiritual effort represented by our attempts to face the *primal trauma* of man, namely death, and all for the sake of a *woman*. So much we all know. But your letter in which you asked leave to forsake the movement, thus prejudicing every single member in it, welded as we all are by sacrificial suicide . . . this was unheard of and provoked a crisis of grave indecision bordering on despair. In the meantime your election had been decided upon by ballot – you are the next, *were* the *next* sacrificial exemplar of the death-confronting fraternity. Your telegram retracting this decision came after the ritual letter had been sent to you. You can imagine the dismay and confusion you have caused the brotherhood."

"But I have not received any letter," cried out Affad from the depths of his misery. "When was it sent? Where was it sent?"

"It had already been despatched when your own communication was received; there was confusion and delay. But the letter of sacrifice containing the details of your death-confrontation and the time allowed you to prepare . . . it was sent to Geneva where you were then, and, it was thought, likely to remain."

So the blow had fallen! He had, after so many years of patience, at last been elected. Extraordinary emotions assailed him now, discharging themselves in his heart so that he felt at one and the same time proud, sorrowful, and in an intermittent way wildly elated, as if the adventure for which he had longed for so long had begun. But then doubts intervened; would it be cancelled in the light of his apostasy? Suddenly deep gloom replaced the elevation of spirit at the very thought.

"I implore you to let me go through with it. Let my retraction be accepted, let me redeem my crime by the act of sacrificial fulfilment according to the vow I took." In the silence he could hear his own heart beating loudly, anxiously. What if this bitter cup should be taken from him, just because of a momentary weakening of his resolve? How remote the painful image of his love seemed at that moment of self-abasement, of cringing self-immolation! Seeing himself with her eyes he realised just how despicable he would have seemed to her could she see him now. And also how amazing, for under the veneer of sophistication and formal culture there now appeared the initial gnostic Manichee born of those long deliberations and fasts and mental exercises. Constance would have been afraid to see him almost grovelling before his Inquisitors, pleading with them to restore his death! What appalling fantasies men harbour – that is what she would think. But he brushed her from his mind like a fly; and now truly he really wanted to die. The whole tide of his disenchantment with the human race and their way of living rose in him and overflowed into a measureless pessimism. And love had made him wish to turn his back upon reality and blinker himself with transitory passion. To wake and sleep with her. To engender a child – *a child!* What a trap he had prepared for himself. Still with his beggar's gesture of the outstretched hand he cried hoarsely, "I implore! I implore!" But in a paradoxical sort of way he was also imploring Constance to forgive him, to release him, to understand the full extent of his religious dilemma. The voice went on: "It is the more painful as all three of us, sent here to make a judgement on you, were originally converted to the gnostic posture by your homilies and your formulations!"

That was the cruellest cut of all! His own converts had become his judges – if that was the word. At any rate from his own point of view the matter of the first importance was to have his retraction accepted; then he must set about finding the fatal letter. It must have been sent in the diplomatic pouch reserved for Red Cross affairs and be somewhere between offices in Geneva.

A long silence had fallen – the three dark figures seemed to have fallen into a temporary inertia. Then the second one said, "The judgement must be debated and voted upon. Other consultations must follow. This cannot be achieved before tomorrow at midday. The result will be communicated to you by Prince Hamid. You should go now and wait upon the judgement which will be neither merciful nor indulgent but just and logical."

The posture had cramped his legs and he rose stiffly to a standing position and unsteadily bowed his thanks to the invisible group. Three pairs of hands briefly rose in farewell and as briefly subsided upon the stone. He groped his way to the door and switched on his pocket torch to light him back through the crypt. Behind him he heard the low murmur of their confabulation begin. What would the upshot of it all be? Surely they must accept his sacrifice as foreseen long ago – the year when three and then five, fellow believers went calmly into infinity armed with the hope, indeed the belief, that their sacrifice turned back the tide of dissolution and offered a pattern of hope to the beleaguered world?

He climbed back into his house, mounting the stairs in dazed exhaustion. He was violently sick. A clock struck three – it was very late. Soon dawn would be breaking. His quiet bedroom . . . the bed had been turned down. Could he sleep, he wondered? Could he sleep, with such great affairs impending? To make sure of the matter he prepared a strong dose of a sleeping draught and with its aid sunk into sleep as if into a cavern; and here came the dreams of the forgotten Constance, memories of their love in all its unexpected variety and tenderness. Everything that he had simply abolished when talking to his judges returned like a tide and swallowed up his emotions. When he awoke it was already past eleven. There were tears on his face, on his cheeks; he indignantly washed them away in the shower, glorying in the swishing water. Then he put on his old rough *abba* instead of the habitual silken dressing-gown and went downstairs to the great glassed-in central hall where the brilliant whiteness of daylight caressed his small but choice collection of statues and the tropical plants which framed the further end leading into the garden. A fountain played – he had always loved the sound of water indoors. There was even a group of brilliant fish. Pastilles of incense burned in the wall niches. He sat himself down at the recently laid table and poured out some coffee. In a little while the Prince would telephone and tell him the verdict of the three, the 'executive cell'. Quietly, as he sat there and listened to the water running, he went back in memory to the remote past when first these gnostic notions had begun to germinate in his mind. Step by step he had been led backwards in chronological time, negation by negation, until he had come up against the hard integument of Greek thought a strange and original manifestation of the human spirit. It had assimilated and modified and perhaps even betrayed these successive waves of esoteric knowledge which, like a tropical fruit, were the harvest of Indian thought, of Chinese thought, of Tibetan thought. He saw these dark waves of culture pouring into Persia, into Iran, and into Egypt, where they were churned and manipulated into linguistic forms which made them comprehensible to the inhabitants of the Middle Eastern lands.

Greece was the sieve, with its worship of light and its unbending propensity for logic and causation. The Greek philosophers, one by one, took over the world-pictures of different peoples and wove them up into self-consistent philosophical systems. Pythagoras took up the Chinese world-system, Heraclitus the Persian, Xenophanes and the Eliatics the Indian, Empedocles the Egyptian, Anaxagoras the Israelite. And finally, in a mind-crushing attempt at synthesis Plato tried to bring together all these foreign influences and harmonise them into a truly Hellenic world-view both spiritual and social, both scientific and vatic . . .

These ideas and memories excited him so much that he got up and walked up and down the hall with his hands behind his back, reliving the thrilling agony he had felt while he first formulated them for himself under the tutorship of old Faraj the philosopher. Yes, but before Plato even, came the wise Mani and his disciple Bardesanes – they were the hinge between the Orient and the Occident. He clasped his hands and felt anew the thrill of his first affirmation of allegiance to the 'pentad' and the 'triad'; in poetic terms these were the five senses and the three orifices. But in fact for the Buddhist psychology it spelt the five *skandas*, bundles of apprehension, reservoirs of impulse! He remembered so well the impressive way Faraj had said, "My son, the Manichean Prince of Darkness combines the forms of five elemental demons: smoke (δαιμον), lion (fire), eagle (wind), fish (water), darkness (δράκων). In Greece his prophet is Pherecyrdes. . . . Out of this mixture of studies and fasts and meditations the Thing had grown and grown until one day a man unknown to him had knocked at the door and gained entry. He was old and dressed like some Coptic tramp, but of great presence. He said simply, "My son, have you considered death, the primal trauma of man?" And Affad had nodded, for the person and the question seemed familiar, as if he had waited a century for this event to occur; and beckoned him to a seat. So the adventure had begun – death as an adventure!

They could not deprive him of his right at this stage. He had earned it by those long solitary years which had so puzzled his fellow-citizens that they had hatched the most extravagant rumours about him, just to account for the fact that he lived alone and had no attachments; the life of a seminarist or monk. They said that he must be a secret homosexual, or impotent, or bewitched, or had taken a vow with a view to entering holy orders! And all to explain why in a city of debauch and casual venery he kept himself apart, though he lived a full enough social and business life. Now he went slowly round his possessions saying goodbye to them one by one, just as a rehearsal, to see how much he was attached to them and how much it would hurt to leave them. He still gloated over them – the obsidian head of a Roman cup-bearer, two cloud puffed *putti*, the skull of a woman covered in gold leaf from a desert tomb. No, but the cord was cut in the most profound sense of the word. He was no longer owned by them. His feelings were sharper when they consulted smaller, more trivial things. On his dressing-table the latch-key Lily had given him, his first toy soldier, a grenadier with no head. One drawer was full of a jumble of small items incomprehensible to any but himself; a dance-book from carnival with his own name filling up every space, written in the hand of Lily. ("I don't want anyone to put their arms round you.") Yes, at times his celibacy had become a fearful burden, specially in springtime when the first dry desert winds struck the capital; it was agony not to have a girl in one's arms, in one's bed. Sometimes in an agony of loneliness he walked down to the dark Corniche to watch the moon rising on the sea. In the darkness they called to one another, the lovers, with names like Gaby, Yvette, Yolande, Marie and Laure. How they ached, the names!

One night he passed a girl alone, standing quite still, looking at the sea, and actually brought himself to speak to her. "Are you alone, Mademoiselle?" She gazed at him for a long moment, as if sizing him up, and then replied in soft, disenchanted tones, "Too much for my liking". They walked quite unhurriedly the length of the Corniche, talking like old friends, and when they reached the outskirts of the town again he asked her to come back to his house with him, for he did not wish to spend another night alone. She hesitated for a moment and then quietly agreed. Together they walked back. When she saw the relative luxury of his home she said, "You must be very rich, then." He replied, "Well, I am a banker by profession." But her reaction was one of relative indifference. She was a gentle, rather passive girl, pleasant-looking rather than pretty, but not vulgar. They had at first spoken Greek, but now it was French. Her name was Melissa, she said, and by now she had warmed to his gentleness and lack of brashness.

The rest seemed to follow naturally and he enjoyed the immense luxury not only of lovemaking but also of sleeping and drowsing beside this gentle and composed and somewhat melancholy woman, who was not a *fille de joie* in the professional sense but something more like a *grisette*. They warmed to each other though neither made any effort to arrange a further meeting. She did not, perhaps, think it was her place to do so. He wanted to write her a cheque, having no cash on him, but she would not take it. "I am with an old Jew who is jealous and goes through my bag. And I couldn't cash it until Monday. Give me two or three of your cigars, the Juliets, he likes cigars. I could say I stole them or bought them." But this did not seem to him adequate. "Melissa, give me your address and I will send you a money order by post." But she did not want to do so. When first they reached the house they had talked and joked, and when he asked if she had never been married she had laughed and slipped the paper ring from his Juliet on to her ring finger and held it up, turning it this way and that as if it had been a real ring with a precious stone in it! "Alas, my family is penniless, I have no dowry." But she did not sound preternaturally sad about it.

In the morning, when she departed with the three cigars for her lover, he found that she had left beside the bathroom wash-basin where she had performed her toilette the paper ring, and beside it the world's oldest contraceptive device, namely a pessary carved out of a small slip of fine sponge and impregnated with olive oil. It was washed now and dry, and as he thought of it, the history of it which stretched back into the remotest corners of Mediterranean mythic lore, he picked it up and together with the ring slipped them both into the drawer of his dressing-table among the other souvenirs of youth. This was now among the objects to which he was saying adieu, and for a brief second he wondered what had happened to the girl, for he had never seen her again after the night spent together. The objects themselves might have come from some Stone Age grave so remote did they seem: yet they had poignance.

These reveries were interrupted by the chirping of the telephone. He awoke as if from a trance and made his way across the hall to hear the voice of the Prince at the other end of the wire – full of relief and suppressed sadness. He said, "They have just rung me up with the result of the whole enquiry. Your retraction has been accepted and your rights have been restored to you . . ." He paused for a long moment, awaiting who knows what reaction from his friend. But Affad stayed stock-still with the receiver to his ear, drinking in the news and still saying not a word. He was like someone who learns that he has won a great lottery, speechless and uncomprehending. For the first time he realised the enormous attraction of death, and the secret lust for it which animates human beings. Fear and lust. In the distant recesses of memory he heard the voice of Constance saying (as she did one day when they were discussing the matter), "But it may be that you are deeply schizoid without knowing it or feeling it!" It had made him laugh at the time, for what could such formulations possibly mean in the context of a reality such as the one he was embracing?

"How marvellous," he said in a low voice, cherishing this sense of voluptuous completeness. The Prince went on, "The letter had already been sent to you when they received your abdication, hence the confusion. Now it is in order again."

"But I received no letter," said Affad.

"It must be in Geneva waiting for you. I think they sent it to the Red Cross pouch – you know all the problems we face today. First the British, that meddlesome fool Brigadier Maskelyne is always prying for British Intelligence, and then the Egyptian police are convinced that we are a subversive political movement . . . So care must be taken. But the letter has been written and the details worked out."

"They did not tell you any details? How long have I got, for example, and where must I expect the last scene to take place?"

"No, they told me nothing. I suppose in Geneva itself, though I don't know when. I have sent an urgent signal to try and trace the letter. It must be in your tray in Geneva but we might as well make sure."

"Who wrote it? Who would know? I would like to know

whether I must say goodbye here and return there or whether I have some months ahead of me."

"Only the letter can tell you that."

"Can't you ask the committee?"

"My dear, I don't know who they are. I was told the little I know by a voice, an anonymous voice. It was someone I did not know, so how could I ask someone? Who?"

"I see." It was very vexatious not to be in full possession of the details; it was like planning a long voyage and not being in possession of the tickets.

"I foresaw your puzzlement," said the Prince, "and I tried to find out myself by telephoning to Samsoun. He was not sure but thought that you would be expected to be present in Geneva for the next few months. And things are more conveniently arranged abroad, as you know. I should act on that assumption until we find the blasted letter and can be sure. Say goodbye to Alexandria leaving you!" It was grim to quote the famous poem at this moment, but the Prince was overwhelmed with sadness at the prospect of losing an irreplaceable friend, and nervous excitement makes one do tactless things. "Yes," said Affad slowly, "I think you are right. I shall do just that, and in my own time. How strange it will feel! See you later in the day." He rang off and went to dress. Then he walked down into the town at his usual leisurely pace, first to drop into the Bourse and renew old acquaintances in their offices, then to study the fluctuations of the market. Everyone was so glad to see him back that for a while he almost forgot the valedictory nature of these visits. People thought that he had come back after a long stay abroad to resume the old life of the banking community of the city. He went to the club to read the newspapers, or such of them as were still alive after the war. There was a Rotary meeting going on upstairs and he made a surprise visit to it, to join in its deliberations and greet other older associates.

That evening he changed into a habitual dinner jacket and joined the Prince's dinner party at the Auberge Bleu to keep up his reputation for pleasant affability: and as he was a good dancer, his reputation as a tolerable ladies' man. Once or twice he caught the Prince staring at him with a sort of hungry, affectionate curiosity, as if he were trying to evaluate his friend's feelings, but Affad had never been demonstrative, his expressions were not easy to decipher. But during a brief exchange he said, "Tomorrow night I am going out to Wady Natrun to see Lily for the last time; may I tell her that she can count on you in the future if she needs help?" The reproachful glance of the Prince told him that his question need not have been asked.

"Will she see you?" he asked.

"I do not know. I will try."

Lily was another preoccupation. Somebody had once asked him at a party, "Who is that girl you were talking to? *The girl with the tears in her voice?*" It expressed the sense of poignant rapture of her tone, a voice swerving like some brilliant bird from register to register. What had become of her soul, her mind, now that her body no longer counted for her – sleeping in some wattle hut in the middle of the desert with only the hideous summer sun for company? He sighed as he thought of the desert. It too was an abstraction like the idea of death – until the life of the oasis made it a brutal reality. Yet what terrible longings the desert bred in its addicts! "Yes, surely she will see me," he told himself under his breath. He said goodnight to his hosts and walked down to the seafront for a breath of air before facing the night. The sea was rough, but playfully so, resounding to a rogue wind from the islands. It dashed itself on the rocks below the Corniche. Few people were about, but here and there was a group of friends returning on foot from some party or other. Once he heard the soft strains of a guitar vibrating in the distance. The museum slumbered in darkness with all its trophies – did the statues manage to doze for a moment during the Alexandrian night? The light in the hall had been left on by the thoughtful Said; he found his way to the kitchen for a late cup of tea which he took up to bed with him; he would have liked to read, but his eyelids felt heavy and as he did not want to lose this valuable predisposition he did nothing but just lay there drinking his tea and watching the shadows on the ceiling and thinking of Constance. What would she be doing at this hour? he wondered.

Soon they would come to the end of the road and she would have to find a new path through the future. It weighed in him, the sadness, but there was also mixed with the emotion a sense of relief and fulfilment. He slid softly, as if down a sand dune, into a harmless, dreamless sleep.

The next evening he took the desert road and drove in the cool of the day along the narrow tarmac road which united the two capitals, Cairo and Alexandria. The heat haze had subsided, the sky was clear with the promise of a ghostly moon to light his return. His anxiety as to whether Lily would see him or not had sharpened today, for he had begun to have new doubts. Night was coming – he could feel the evening damps rising to his cheeks as the open car traversed the dunes towards the distant green splash which marked the site of the oasis. He would perhaps arrive before the great portals were closed upon the darkness, perhaps not. It did not matter, he could always knock, he told himself.

The monastery gradually rose up out of the sand with its curiously barbaric atmosphere – as if it stood somewhere much more remote, perhaps on the steppes of Middle Asia? The cluster of beehive buildings were glued together in a vast complex of brownish stone: pumice and plaster and whatnot, and the colour of wattle smeared with clay. This light, friable type of material offered excellent insulation against both desert heat and also the cold of the darkness during the winter.

The palm groves stood there, silently welcoming, with their weird hieratic forms, benignly awkward. But the great doors had been shut and he was forced to lift the heavy knocker and dash it upon the booming wood once or twice and to swing upon the thick bellrope which set up a remote interior jangling in the distant recesses of the place. At last a monk opened and interrogated him, and having given the name of Yanna correctly he was allowed to send him a message and to take a chair in the waiting-room with its dense smell of candlewax and incense.

The principal Coptic father of the monastery had been once a banker, but for many years now had retired to this life of silence and contemplation, though he ruled the place with an iron hand and vaunted the efficiency of its activities. He was completely bald and had a heavy, Chinese-looking countenance which contained, deeply embedded, two eyes of penetration and pertness, always twinkling on the edge of laughter. Affad greeted him with affectionate familiarity and explained that he had come on the offchance of an interview with Lily as he was planning to go on a long journey and wished to see her before he went away: also to give her up-to-date news of the child . . . Yanna debated and sighed as he did so, shaking his brown dome of a head doubtfully. He said, "Nobody has seen her for ages now; food is left and the dish is emptied and put back outside her hut, so we know she is alive, that is all. But she was in a bad way, a significant way. She once wrote me a message saying, 'I have begun to see colours with my mouth and hear sounds with my eyes, everything is confused. If I take a pencil in hand I make letters a foot high. I must retire and cure myself again.'" They gazed at one another, reflecting. "The best would be just to go and try. She can only refuse, you can only go away after all." He crossed the room to the wall upon which there was a large framed picture of the oasis with the grouping of the buildings clearly marked, thinning away into the desert where there were the cells, mere wattle shelters which housed those who had chosen to live as solitary anchorites. There were also a few lean-to shelters for sheep against the desert winds. He placed his finger on one of the star-shaped huts and said, "There! I will give you the monk Hamid who takes food, he will show you the way; but my friend, if she is unwilling don't insist, I implore you!" Affad looked reproachfully at his friend and said, "Of course not – why do you say that?"

"I'm sorry. It was out of place. I apologise."

The old monk who was the night-janitor of the monastery now appeared bearing in his hand a dark-lantern and a wattle basket with some fruit and a bowl of rice. He bowed and grunted his assent when he had received the orders and, turning, led the way across the complex of silent buildings and thence through a large lemon grove which, like an outpost, opened directly on to desert dunes with here and there a fringe of palms.

It was quite a stumble across the sands and Affad could not help noticing with admiration the curious ease of movement of his companion: his walk was a sort of glide across the difficult terrain. The lantern with its single candle seemed on the point of going out all the time; but a frail horn of moon was rising through the dense fur of the night mists. So they came at last to one of the remotest cells beyond which lay nothing – just the uncompromising sea of sand curling and flowing away into the empty sky. In such a place the sight of a stone or of a distant bird of prey would stand out from the whole of nature like a sun-spot. He shivered with a pleasurable distaste as he thought of life here, how it must be; to be alone with one's thoughts here, and *nothing else to distract you away from thinking them*. The old man grunted, put down the lantern some way from the wooden door and gave a strange hoarse cry, as if to some domestic animal: a sort of "Hah!" or "Hey!"

For a while there was no response and then they heard a

shuffling noise, as of a broom sweeping up dead leaves, or of someone rustling old parchment, old newspapers. But no voice. The janitor advanced to the door, and after placing his ear to it, drew back and said hoarsely, "Someone is here to see you." At the same moment he beckoned Affad to come and stand beside him, and by the same token, to make himself known. Affad did not know what to say, everything had flown out of his mind. He said at last, "Lily! Listen! It is I."

There was a further rustling sort of commotion and then the door opened violently and a gaunt, ragged figure appeared, shielding its face from the dim light and chattering with excitement like a sort of huge monkey. He cried out her name again and the chattering subsided a little while her voice – such as it was, for the sound was as disembodied as if it came from some kind of instrument – called to the old janitor, "Go and leave me!" And the old man, taking up his lantern with a submissive reverence, glided away into the surrounding night. Now the light was indeed dim, yet he did not dare to reach for the little electric torch he always carried in his pocket. She was like some rare bird which might be disturbed by the light, might disappear in a panic. How did she look now, after all this time? He could not guess.

It was as if she had lip-read his mind for she said slowly, "I wonder how we look now, after all this time?" They stood listening to each other's breathing, just their antennae touching, so to speak. Then he said, "I have a light, if you wish to see." Actually he wished to see her, to evaluate how she was, from her eyes. Silence again. "Shall I show you?" She said nothing but just stood, so he slowly reached back into his pocket for the little torch which always aided him plant his latchkey correctly. He held it above his head like a douche and switched it on so that the light flowed down over his countenance; at the same time raising his head. She gasped. "It does not look like you at all," she said. "Not at all."

He was dismayed and a little astonished because it seemed that she was talking about someone else, to somebody else. He had the sudden impression that he was now impersonating somebody he did not know, had not met. "What is your name?" she asked, with a touch of peremptory sternness, increasing his discomfort, his sense of being there under false pretences. "Surely you know," he said. "Surely, Lily!"

She burst into tears, but very briefly; after a single cry the current was switched off, so to speak, and she knuckled her eyes free and said humbly, "I have forgotten. Not speaking for long, my memory has gone." Her wild look of sadness was replaced by one of savage expectation. She took his wrists and shook them softly. "Shall I guess?" she said slowly. He nodded. "Yes, Lily, guess." She bowed her head on her breast in deep contemplation. Then she gave a small snort and said, "It is like a gigantic crossword puzzle, only instead of words just sounds to be filled in and colours!" She was speaking of reality, he quite understood. It made him feel helpless and morbidly sad. "O God, why can't you remember? Can't you remember when you dropped the basket and all the eggs were broken – *every last one?*" She gave a cry of amazement, youthful and lyrical, her face cast up to the sky as she pronounced the word, the elusive word: "*Sebastian!* At last I have got it. O my darling! How could I?" And now she was really crying and in his arms, her fragility made all the more striking by the tension, the electric current flowing through her body like wind through the foliage of a tree. He held her humbly and with pity and a wild desire to make amends to her for the shortcomings of the world which had allotted her only half a human mind, but not (cruelly) withdrawn the capacity to love! He groaned in the inside of his own mind, groaned. It was stupid, he knew. One always feels that one should be able to cure the whole world. That one is to blame for everything, every iniquity. It was a form of false pride, he supposed.

He felt that what was needed at that moment was to give her confidence, and so with a kind of necessary innocence he sat down on the ground before the hut, pocketing his torch. And after a moment of indecision so did she. So they sat in the dust facing each other, like Arab children. Now her breathing had become less laboured, and her fingers had ceased to tremble, so he felt that he could embark upon a recital of his adventures since last they had met. Nor did he omit anything, speaking about his attachment to Constance with a kind of puzzled sincerity which seemed to her very moving, for she stifled a sob and put two fingers sympathetically upon his wrist. He told her that Constance was to try and evaluate the position of their son in medical terms and decide upon what treatment, if any, was best for the case. But even as he spoke she shook her head softly from side to side as if she had already made up her own mind about the matter, and that it did not offer much hope.

And then about himself. "I have received my own orders as well; you know that for some time I was quite expecting them – well, now the die is cast, though for the moment I haven't got the actual details. But this will be our last meeting, of that I am sure. So I must thank you for everything, and for having put up with my shortcomings as you did. It was not your fault that things turned out the way they did." O dear! It was the truth and yet it sounded terribly prosy when put into words; and why the devil did he have this sense of contrition? Had it been his fault? Lily was like a butterfly born with only one wing – otherwise perfect in every way. The fatal handicap stood in the way of fulfilment – or perhaps simply changed its prerogatives. She would sit there in darkness now, perhaps for life after life, gazing at a hole in space throughout the full length and breadth of time. He could see her whole future of darkness in his mind's eye – as if she stood on the bridge of a liner; the night was a liner, slowly travelling through absolute darkness towards an undisclosed goal somewhere in the darkness ahead. "Well," she said humbly at last, "So you must go at last. We must all go." And she gave a sigh full of world weariness and passed into a kind of compassionate silence, still touching his wrist with her fingers. After a long time he stirred and rose, and they embraced and stood latched one to the other in a final decisive gesture. Kissed also. It was like kissing the face of a rag doll. Then he left her.

He drove himself back across the desert in a state of dejection and exhaustion, glad of the car's tinny radio which accompanied his thoughts with the monotonous ululations of Arabic music unwinding its quartertone spools forever upon the moonlit night. His headlights put up startled desert creatures – were they hares? They fled so fast into the surrounding darkness that he could not say for sure. And then at last the dispiriting city of chromium lusts and avarice and boredom! How well the music illustrated its suffocating monotony, its limitations of growth, squeezed between two deserts! He would be glad to get away again. Abruptly he snapped off the radio and allowed the swishing desert silence to fill the hull of his car. It was late. He was exhausted by so much fervent thought. The house was dark except for the hall light. He felt suddenly sad and mateless. He lay down on his bed fully dressed and went to sleep at once, only to be woken by the discreet knock of Said as he came in bearing a cup of early morning tea. He drank it with relief and treated himself to a long hot shower before going downstairs to where his breakfast awaited him beside the small lilypond with its whispering water.

At ten the phone rang and a somewhat irascible Prince asked him where the devil he had been, "because I was trying to reach you last evening and there was no reply". Affad explained; but he was intrigued by the note of concern, almost of alarm, in the Prince's voice as he went on, "I spend almost the whole day on the phone to Geneva – you will imagine the difficulties, the bad lines and so on – in the hope of finding out about your famous letter. It was delivered to your office, and thence taken by Cade to the clinic, thinking you were with Aubrey, but you had gone. Now comes the funny part: Aubrey gave it to Constance, thinking that she would certainly be seeing you. But apparently she did not, or forgot it. At any rate she seems to have it, but after a series of calls to her consulting rooms I managed to get Schwarz who tells me that she has gone on leave of absence, to have a rest. Of the letter he knows nothing. It's to be presumed that she still has it?" Affad was puzzled by the tone of the Prince for it conveyed a notion of alarm, which did not seem to match the rather commonplace facts of the case. After all, a letter had gone astray, but was not lost. He said, "You sound sort of strange."

"I am a little put out," admitted the Prince, "and I will tell you why. When I managed to get through to Aubrey and he said that he had handed it to her he said that she had been angry and depressed, and said that she had half a mind to put it into the fire or tear it up unread. You see, she disapproves very strongly in . . . well, in *us*, all we stand for. I wish to hell he had not been so indiscreet. But you see that if she were to do anything impulsive like that it would constitute a sort of technical miscarriage vis-à-vis the central committee. I could not foresee the reaction, but once more you would come under fire." Affad groaned and agreed. "I would have liked to tell Constance direct that any attempt to interfere with the course of . . . well, justice, historical justice, in a sense, might put you in a gravely prejudicial position . . . But now she has gone away somewhere and we don't know for how long. I have left a message with her colleague Schwarz, but he is a pretty vague fellow like all analysts. Anyway I can do no more."

"Thank you, anyway," said Affad. "I see no undue cause for worry. But of course once a woman disturbs a sequence of events by a rash act . . ."

"Exactly," said the Prince. "It always makes me nervous when a woman intervenes. Things usually get into a tangle. At any rate, for the moment there is no undue cause for our fears. Have you made any plans yourself?"

"I haven't yet said goodbye in Cairo so I plan to spend a few days there this week. Back Saturday."

THREE

Inner Worlds

AS FOR CONSTANCE, SHE HAD AT LAST TAKEN THE ADVICE of Schwarz and left for the little lake house which they used for weekends of leave. It lay in a sunken garden and was built over a boat-house containing the precious motor-boat of Schwarz, which he had christened *Freud.* There was also a tiny skiff which they used when they wished to sunbathe on the lake or to visit the local *auberge* for lunch or dinner. It was a delectable corner and there was no telephone – a fact which set off its quality of seclusion and quiet. As ideal for work as for rest, then.

But in her present disturbed mood it would have been hard to think of rest, so she had done what she had so often done before, namely taken her work with her in the form of the medical dossier which the central clinic had built up out of their investigations of Affad's son; a document which depressingly reflected the objective medical view of the child as "a case". It lay before her on the rough deal table together with her type-writer and a cluster of pencils and notebooks. She shrank from it somehow, for she could foresee its dispiriting evaluations of human misery, and the inflated vocabulary which could hardly disguise the almost total ignorance in which their science lay shrouded. Nevertheless. One must begin somewhere, one must make an effort to understand, the hunt for exact observation was their only *raison d'être.* She could hear the cautious voice of Schwarz cutting into her thoughts to warn her, "Yes, but method, while desirable, must remain an art and not dwindle into a barren theology – the sort of superstition upon which dead universities exist!"

Okay. Okay. *Symbiotic child psychosis with marked*

autistic traits. As she read the portrait of the small staring face in the sailor hat, fervent in its withdrawn impavidness, gazed out upon her from the slowly gliding limousine. It was of course the face of Affad in miniature that she watched.

> The child was referred by a hospital where he had been kept under observation for three weeks of tests at the request of his father and the child's grandmother; the mother, who had a long record of psychic upheavals punctuated by ordinary periods during which she resumed her responsibilities, exhibiting a normal but hypertense relationship to the family circle when she was at home. But during periods of collapse or stress she herself returned to her home in Egypt and had herself committed as a voluntary patient for rest and treatment. The evolution of the boy's childhood seems to have been normal and regular, but after the mother's first disappearance for long from the scene during his sixth year, he fell ill with a fever which resisted accurate diagnosis, but which kept him in bed for several months during which the present traits slowly evolved. The behaviour pattern was sufficiently striking to prompt parental anxiety and the father sought medical aid. The case was referred to my care and a fairly detailed and intensive period of observation and evaluation followed, during which I saw the child for several hours a day. His grandmother was permitted to stay in the hospital with him, though he himself exhibited neither alarm nor curiosity and stayed sunk in the apathy of his condition.

The report had been written by an old friend and fellow-student of Constance, a wise and experienced neurologist not lacking in insight and affection, with children of her own; and it was extremely detailed, though as always with such a subject, consistently tentative. She heard Schwarz again: "Despite such a river of verbiage we know damn all about the human condition either in health or in sickness. Yet we must slog along." Slog was the word! Constance made herself some tea and returned to the thoughtful and painstaking document of her friend.

> The standard preliminary tests showed no trace of anything pathological. There seemed to be no history of lues or any other family illness in the background. Cerebral computer tomography registered normal states.
>
> Up till the time of his illness which could have been touched off by the crisis of his mother's departure, his development had been somewhat retarded as to speech and the making of sounds; but not sufficiently marked to warrant real anxiety – some children are slow to learn to speak. But from the illness onwards his autistic behaviour grew so marked as to prompt a question as to whether he were not actually deaf and not responsive to sound-signals. Yet this did not seem to be the case for at some loud noises he turned the head, but very slowly, and his look was blank and incurious. Sometimes he stood quite still with eyes narrowed as if he were listening to some inner noise, though his reactions remained expressionless and stony. He submitted to caresses with equal indifference, and if a human face approached his would look away or look through it into some imaginary place, as if something or someone were waiting for him there. His great physical beauty makes it easy to be fanciful about him. But he was like a mechanism which proves defective, had stuck definitively at a certain stage in the building. With both eye-contact and physical contact lost one became somewhat hesitant about an explicit diagnosis of the case. I myself alternated between notions of cerebral damage, pure autism, shock and

hyperkinetic syndrome: since whenever he did move the procedure was almost ataxic in its lack of coordination, though always violent and directed towards some inanimate object around him, into which he often sank his teeth before dropping it and then standing still, to stare at a wall or door with total expressionlessness. He did not behave destructively with his hands, tearing things apart, but simply sank his teeth into them, and then dropped them.

His grandmother with whom he lived was herself a somewhat dramatic old lady, and seemed disposed to help, but owing to her defective French and Italian did not seem able to provide much understanding which might be of medical aid to a would-be physician. The boy was named Affad after his father, a businessman who came frequently to see him but lived in semi-permanence in Egypt and did not reside in Geneva. The old lady lived in great luxury in her own lakehouse with several servants, a large private limousine as well as an expensive motor-boat for outings, on which the little boy always accompanied her after being carefully dressed for the occasion in true Levantine style. The family came originally from Alexandria in Egypt.

In these circumstances the child lived a strange non-life, or a life of total non-cooperation despite the presence of kindly servants. His vast playroom was full of toys which he ignored, even the musical ones, like the toy piano and drum and xylophone which would normally tempt a child. Of course with both father and mother absent there was a lack of family atmosphere about his life, but many children suffer such conditions without becoming ill. This could be a subsidiary reason but did not seem to be central. Nor could his father offer any clues; he was a somewhat effete and withdrawn figure, fashionably and even elegantly dressed, but overcame the first impression of insipidity and proved extremely articulate, though of course completely in the dark as to the child. His own medical history offered none either, and he seemed depressed and concerned about this highly intractable condition which had, as he put it, rendered his child as silent as a mummy. I obtained his active agreement to venture upon a series of tentative visits to the child with a view to trying to penetrate this mask of impassivity, or at least come to a definite conclusion as to the causes. I spent over an hour in his presence about three times a week, just to observe his habits, however passive they might be. He was taken out on the lake sometimes in the big motorlaunch, dressed up and clean. He liked to sit and trail one hand in the water, though without any evident pleasure. The other excursion was in the limousine which went slowly along the lakeside for an hour or so. He sat looking at the passers-by and the houses, but saying nothing, impassive.

He does not refuse food but he has still to be fed, although old enough to feed himself; nor does he show any preference as to dishes. He goes through the actions of eating with indifference. He sleeps restlessly and sometimes groans in his sleep or whimpers and has been known to suck his sheet – but this is a fairly normal suckling hangover like thumb-sucking; one is tempted to think that it would be too easy to assume his condition to be the result of shock at his mother's departure. I would say rather that the shock touched off a more deeply based anxiety historically situated in the remoter past, and was concerned with his suckling problems. I suspected that the mother might have been guilty of depriving the child of its milk either from distaste for the whole business, like so many mothers; or simply had broken off the suckling period in favour of the bottle at too early a stage. Of course this is a traditional view after Klein, yet it is rather puzzling that he showed no disturbances over eating now, that his whole condition seemed to be independent of a food problem.

Here the dossier came to an end and there followed some notes in the hand of Schwarz which began:

> By ill luck this unsatisfactory preliminary sketch could not be amplified as the therapist was forced to return to Canada on duty and owing to staff shortages we could not allocate another for many months, so that the situation was allowed to drift and at the time of writing has not markedly changed. All the elements described here remain constant, and the life led by the child maintains its steady rhythm. I think it desirable that we try and penetrate a little further into the obscurity of his condition. There are a number of things which have not been tried; for example a pet, say a kitten. It is hard to resist a kitten playing with wool or a rolling ping-pong ball. Harder to resist the advances of a puppy. Then, what effect if any have images? Images projected on the nursery wall could be tried, just to see whether they raise the tone of his response. What about music while he sleeps . . .? I throw out these suggestions at random. I think, however, that since you have gone as far as to promise your friend a consultation you should perhaps take the place of the therapist and continue the portrait of this (in my own view, looking in from the outside) classical autism!

The dossier was marked in her name and with the classification numeral of her post-office box. What should be done, she wondered, that had not already been done by her more experienced colleague?

Wind rose off the lake and whirled the shutters closed; she set them to rights and after checking the moorings of the skiff set about cooking her frugal dinner in the cosy kitchen with its wooden walls and waterscape. The moralist in her frowned a little at herself, at her eagerness to come to the rescue of the child, for she felt her intention to be not quite pure, not quite disinterested. After all, had it not been the child of Affad ... what would she have done? Most likely deserted it in favour of more interesting cases? Perhaps. "You are still showing your vulnerability," she told herself, and with the thought a wave of hatred swept over her—hatred for Affad and the appalling game of cat's cradle he was playing with her attachment. Damn him! And damn that collection of dismal death-worshippers projecting their infantile death-wish out of a ruined Egypt! "I thought the Germans were infantile enough," she said to herself, "and that the Mediterranean races were older and wiser ... what a fool! How naive can you be?"

All this self-recrimination did not however help her to come to a decision about her clinical role in the affair of the child. She would sleep on it and decide in the morning whether to go through with it or simply to pass it to some other therapist. There were several skilful and devoted people she could think of who were quite as capable as she was, and would be glad to round off the portrait of the robot-child. It cost her a pang to think this, however, and she slept badly, dreaming of him with a fervent sadness.

In the morning she woke and at once recalled the description of Affad as a "somewhat effete and withdrawn figure". This annoyed her, though the feeling was, she knew, utterly irrational. But her own new appearance was pleasing, it was part of the attempt to rehabilitate herself in her own eyes, to rise phoenix-wise from the ashes of this destructive and barren attachment. She had bought the fur coat and some handsome winter gear, she had changed her perfume and she had allowed her hairdresser to alter the style of her hair and wave it differently. It really became her very well – and here there was nobody to see it, to admire it! "Serve you right," she said vindictively to the shade of the departed "effete and withdrawn" one. But she had not been able to resist dropping into the office to seek the approval of her colleague. His reaction was most stimulating. "God! Constance, you look ten years younger and just fallen in love again – how I wish *that* were true!"

In a way, so did she. But the business of sick-leave had been settled and underneath her war-paint lurked the old nightmare of fatigue. He saw the dossier under her arm and nodded his approval of her intentions. In the meantime they were proposing to place Mnemidis under prolonged sedation to see whether a simple rest might not alter his disposition. She felt less badly about leaving the case to Schwarz, who was quite obviously not the therapist to handle it; yet she also regretted her own absence because of the intrinsic fascination of the case itself. Schwarz sensed this and said, "Don't worry about Mnemidis. He is in a pious stage at the moment and has borrowed all the books he can lay hands on. When he next appears on vaudeville it will be in scenes from the Bible I should suppose. *Aber*, what a freak!"

The silence of the little house was broken only by the lapping of the lake water at the wooden jetty. The sun came out and enabled her to move her books and papers on to the lawn which was kept neatly trimmed by a visiting gardener who was invisible except on Mondays. She slept, woke, and slept again. Ate a dazed meal, and was overtaken by a real fatigue now which could only be purged by a siesta which prolonged itself until the night was falling. It seemed that the accumulated weariness of centuries was expressing itself through this long slumber and that she would never be free of it. But on the second day the weight was sloughed, and on the succeeding morning she woke early and on an impulse plunged into the lake – a shock like diving through an icy mirror. She groaned with anguished joy as she towelled herself back into rosy warmth and padded to the cosy kitchen for her breakfast. The rest had done the trick; she had more or less shaped out her line of action over the child. Still in her dressing-gown she drank coffee and ran swiftly through his very unsatisfactory dossier. Then she took her car and motored to the nearest hamlet which boasted a post office and telephoned to the mansion on the lake. A servant answered her and in a short time she heard the deep but uncertain tones of the old lady asking her what she wanted. When Constance gave her name, however, the old lady gave an "Ouf!" of relief and said, "We have been waiting for you for days. I thought perhaps that you had forgotten . . ." Constance sounded suitably shocked as she repeated the word: "*Forgotten?* How could I?"

They elected to meet at teatime on the same afternoon and by the time Constance had parked her car at the gate-house over the water she had no need to ring the bell for the old lady was already in the garden waiting for her behind the grille. She fluttered a white handkerchief in a sort of furtive signal, as if to an accomplice, and came towards the gate almost on tiptoe. "I am so *glad* you have come!" she said in her histrionic gasping way; she had a trick of rolling her eyes as she spoke which invested her speech with a sort of subdued frenzy. It conveyed urgency, and also confusion. It was very Latin.

But when they had shaken hands and looked each other up and down there came a moment of relief, of relaxation, almost as if on both sides the encounter had been somewhat dreaded. The old woman now became serious and stepping back drew herself up and settled her features anew into a severely unforgiving expression, as if calling herself to order after having shown an excess of feeling.

"What will you do?" she said hoarsely, and Constance

shaking her head, replied: "For the moment gain *your* confidence and begin to watch him quietly."

"We are just going out for a drive – *the* drive: perhaps you would care to come with us?" It was a good chance to infiltrate herself into the pattern and she at once accepted, at once followed the old lady through the herb garden with its miniature maze to the garage where already the black limousine waited with a gaitered and helmeted chauffeur at the wheel. He had already thrown the switch which rolled back the garage doors. "His nanny will bring Affad down," explained the old lady, as she allowed the old chauffeur to help her into a warm dark overcoat. "She won't be long."

Nor was she. She appeared quite soon and tried in passing to let the child attempt the marble staircase, but he was so slow that she finally swept him up into her arms and moved towards them, smiling a welcome. She was a fresh-complexioned and rather pretty Swiss girl and Constance already knew that she had her nursing degree and was fully in the counsels of the doctors; moreover she was most eager and willing to help. They exchanged smiles full of conspiratorial warmth and Constance bent briefly to kiss the impassive small face of the boy, who took no atom of interest in their movements or intentions, so familiar to him was the routine drive round the lake edge. He sat beside the old lady, stiffly upright, and with one hand upon her forearm; the two girls sat immediately in front on the fold-out seats. The chauffeur, who was separated from them by glass, checked the speaking tube to make sure that messages would reach him correctly, and switched on the radio in a very subdued manner. They moved off to the faint strains of a Strauss waltz, a strange, disembodied sound which did not disturb the nescience of the child who sat looking out upon the world without curiosity or elation. His little dark face was like that of some great bored plenipotentiary making a familiar state progress through a familiar country, a familiar ritual. Withdrawn as a Buddha he sat, watching the alien world from his perch in the absolute. There was no conversation of a general sort. Constance watched the little boy discreetly in the mirror but the observation revealed nothing, suggested nothing. She must talk to the nanny; and this she arranged sotto voce, suggesting a rendezvous in town where they might exchange views. She already felt that the old lady could contribute little to their debate except expressions of her own intense anxiety, and there was no point in this. On the other hand Constance did not wish to seem to operate behind her back, so to speak. So she broached the subject, pleading a discussion of technical matters, and to her surprise the point was taken without demur; so that the following day the nurse met her at the "*Renon*" for a coffee and a discussion.

She had read the dossier and indeed knew Schwarz already in another context. "Can I tell you what I think of it?" asked Constance, seeing that the girl looked rather doubtful about it when it was mentioned, though she seemed not to want to pronounce upon it in any definite way. "Yes, please!" she replied, and Constance said, "I am not very keen on kittens and toys which make noises; it is not just a question of motor response one is looking for, but a reaction at a deeper level, which can only come from inside himself. How can we help that?" The look of relieved delight on the girl's face changed it utterly; she clapped her hands with delight. "*Exactly* what I thought! No clever tricks for us. I am glad you think so too. There must be subtler ways of waking him. But I am *delighted*. I know we can work together now."

It was a great relief to Constance to find a willing and enthusiastic helper in a common cause; she had feared both jealousy and incompetence in the nursemaid, and neither fear was justified. She was able straight away to arrange her own times of duty and also to launch into a long and detailed list of questions as to the child's reactions to sleep, to food, to hot baths, to massage, and so on. There was little enough to be gleaned, for the subject showed neither special preference nor any really significant aversions. He was simply absent from his shell, his body was simply a package, an appendage. Yet he was painfully like his father in physical structure, with the long head and the same shape of eyes: only his were stone-dead whereas those of Affad senior were both hurt and also wily and amused. She could not help making the comparison when she helped the nurse undress the little one and then lower him into the warm bath in which he lay quite still like a small absorbed frog, listening – for one could not say thinking or feeling. At times waves of despair overcame her. Yet this change of patient, change of objective, brought her fresh energy and enthusiasm, and it was with pleasure that she motored the forty or so kilometres thrice a week now to assume her new role as assistant nanny.

For the first two weeks she did nothing beyond her routine duties of caring and surveying her charge. He looked up when she came into the room sometimes but there was no curiosity, no tone in his look, and for a long while she sat, copying his breathing and attempting to influence him mentally. Sometimes, for a brief moment, he would allow an idea to infiltrate the obscurity of his condition and might perform a parody of rising to walk a few steps with an involuntary clumsiness which might end in a fall. Or else he might pick up a toy and gaze at it in an unseeing way before raising it to his mouth to bite before he dropped it on the floor and resumed his wall-gazing. But very gradually, and with professional stealth, Constance advanced towards a body-contact such as an occasional accidental embrace, or simply a pat on the shoulder; she also developed a small array of daily habits herself which she put on exhibition, so to speak, for his sake: such as drinking a little milk from a plastic mug, combing out her hair, and so on. With these she hoped gradually to draw him towards a familiarity with the circumstantial, and to break his psychic reverie – for after all he was not asleep, he was breathing. He was just not fully alive, that was all. Somewhere there might be a switch. But all this with the greatest precaution and sans haste or impetuousness. It was important to give him the notion that nobody cared because they liked him as he was – they would not wish to influence him! All this slow acting-out seemed interminable and it was almost two months before there were the first signs of contact, but by then Constance had enlarged her own sphere of expression – she was now free to hum, to whistle, to stroke him, to move him about by hand, pick him up, even at long last to sit for long silences with her arm round him, crooning and sometimes breathing on his cheek. Her existence had dawned on him, he was aware of her for sometimes now he smiled and lifted his cheek to feel her blowing softly upon it. At times, too, he lay in her arms with a cryptic expression of enjoyment, closing his eyes, specially if there was music.

Then one day the magical weeping started, the fruitful tears began to flow; yet she was not sure of the mechanism which operated this notable and triumphant departure from the habitual nescience and withdrawal. But happen it did, and at a most awkward time, for she was all dressed up to go to a reception in the town, in order to help Schwarz who was the guest of honour of an International Psychological Association which had given him an important award, not to mention a silver medal for his work in analysis. But the Swiss girl was delayed and Constance had agreed to stay on with Affad for longer than usual.

It was not the fact that she was in a new costume that set the tone for this encounter – for he seemed to show no particular interest, though he smiled faintly to show that she was welcome, and allowed himself to be caressed and even picked up without demur. Yet sitting in her lap he lay back and showed signs of fatigue, yawning and rubbing his eyes. One hand seemed accidentally to touch her hair, and then suddenly move to her face with fingers spread, and apparently with an aggressive intent, as if to plant them in her eyes. But the impulse waned. The threatening quality was new, though. He whimpered as if he wanted to be released, yawned, and even kicked a little, but she held him firmly in order to let him declare himself more fully; evolve and fix the rather vague emotion. But his eyes were clearer, and their focus was more profound and direct, with a quality of alarm – no, the word is too strong – anxiety, in them. He listened to her talk and humming with a new attention, he seemed poised as if upon a new slope down which he had never glided before. He gave a small moan and opened his throat wide, though nothing came forth except a pitiful clicking, dry and incoherent. It was like a yawn which had got stuck. Then suddenly – it was as if the whole of reality rushed in like a Niagara of feeling – suddenly the weeping started, weeping of such violence and abandon that it was as if his little psyche had exploded like a bomb and was on the point of disintegration. She held him tight, as if to hold the shattered fragments together against total dispersion, held him fiercely in her sheltering arms, rocking him slightly from side to side and almost keening his name, the name of her absent lover: "Affad . . . Affad!" It was to congratulate him passionately for this wonderful departure in the direction of the norm. She felt the tears start to her own eyes, but it was important to remain cool in the observation tower of her reason, the better to evaluate the meaning and the possibilities inherent in this new behaviour.

Meanwhile he wept and screamed with all his might as if to rid himself in one cathartic expenditure of all the demons which had held him spellbound for so long, and part of the screaming let loose waves of aggression which made him kick and choke and storm and grind his teeth. This savage gust of anger alternated with waves of almost inhuman despair; he seemed about to shatter into a million fragments, to disperse, to melt. Only the warm and determined ceinture of her arms offered his psyche the chance to contain its woe and reorder the disturbed torrents of the affect flowing out of his very soul. She had never as yet heard anything like it in her professional career, though in the long and tedious confessional work associated with her trade weeping was common enough. But this inarticulate discharge had a fury and despair which was quite unique. It went on and on until it seemed he would come to the end of his voice as well as his strength.

She put him down on the floor and all of a sudden the weeping stopped, as if turned off like a tap, and the child slumped groggily back into a reminiscence of his previous role of absence and wall-gazing; but now he was beside himself with exhaustion, and when she picked him up again he at once went off into a further paroxysm of weeping, as if overcome anew with despair, the uprooting despair of the primal wound whose depth she could not as yet evaluate. Still carrying him, and he was quite heavy, she took him to the luxurious bathroom and turned on the tap to run him a warm relaxing bath. He allowed himself to be undressed while lying on the bed, still expressing a now voiceless weeping. And even when it had started to peter away into the noiselessness of utter exhaustion the face kept the hard fixity of the primal howl, so that (with closed eyes) it resembled something like a tiny Greek tragic mask. He lay so still in the water that he might have been dead; softly and sweetly she sang to herself in a small absorbed voice as she propelled him very slowly back and forth in the bath.

She wrapped him softly in the great perfumed bath-towel and then powdered him with talc before putting him to bed in the quiet bedroom with its faithful night-light burning – a tiny Christmas tree lighted by electric bulbs. Here he seemed at last to cave in, to succumb to a profound slumber, completely extenuated. For a while he turned hither and thus with a trace of his former restlessness, and then turned on his side and like a ship going down, nosedived into sleep. But he did one thing that he had never done before – he thrust his thumb into his mouth. It was an archaic gesture which suggested a fruitful and deep regression to some place of psychic hurt – like someone fingering the scar tissue, the cicatrice of an old wound. As she sat beside him and watched quietly her hopes rose for his restoration to the human world. But she frowned as she thought of the elder Affad, of his delight and perhaps gratitude: had her motives been entirely disinterested? Was it on these grounds . . .? But she shook her head sharply to banish the thought and then looked at her watch. There was half an hour before the Swiss girl came back on duty. He slept so soundly that it might have been possible to tiptoe away, but she did not wish to risk it in case there was some new and fruitful departure in behaviour to be studied. She crossed the room to the day-book and entered a few notes which she would afterwards expand into a case-history, dictating it on to her magnetophone before handing it to her typist. The time passed quickly and by the time the Swiss girl tiptoed into the room she had finished and was ready to polish herself up for the party and take her leave. As she did so she communicated the events of the afternoon and evening to the girl, who showed great delight at the news of a deviation in behaviour. "It might be the beginning of a radical shift," Constance admitted, "But we must be patient and not force."

But she herself was joyfully optimistic and so fully absorbed in her thoughts that she drove extremely badly, and when she got to the town had trouble parking. But she was not too late, and Schwarz's relief was very pleasant to experience; not less, she was forced to admit to herself, the obvious admiration of his colleagues. The new hair-style was a distinct success – that was something pleasurable to experience. But as soon as she could get Schwarz alone she told him excitedly about the events of the afternoon. He whistled with surprise and delight. "What a break-through," he said. "Maybe your original diagnosis was almost right – *histoire de biberon!* What luck if he can find his way back like an electrician going back along a wire to find and seal a break. . . . You are lucky, Constance! I never have these sharp cathartic changes, dammit! But the important thing is the whole continuity – I hope he keeps on until he discharges the whole weight of the trauma. If he does tomorrow and for a while, *please* phone me. I want to know." To her surprise, and indeed a certain mortification, she almost started to cry herself, but managed to check the impulse as she blew her nose. It was a poor advertisement for a cool and scientific therapist, she told herself bitterly.

Schwarz had done a tour of the room and had finally drifted back to her side again with his replenished whisky. "By the way," he said, "I almost forgot to tell you. I am having difficulty defending your privacy, endless telephone calls keep coming in – no, not from Affad, but from the Prince, for example asking where you were and for how long? I said you were on sick leave for at least two months, and away from the country. Is that all right?" She was a little cast down that Affad himself had sent no message, but reproved the sentiment immediately. "Of course," she said, "I owe nobody anything, I am quite free am I not?"

"They are worried about a letter addressed to Affad which came in the Red Cross pouch and which you apparently have; I can't profess to tell you what *that* is all about but he sounds very concerned, asking if you have destroyed it, or opened it or what the hell you have done with it. What do I say?"

She felt herself blushing slightly. Schwarz's glance was a trifle quizzical, although in the matter of Affad he was not fully in her confidence. "If the Prince asks again, please give him my love and tell him that the letter in question was misdirected by

Aubrey Blanford's stupid servant and I took charge of it, hoping to see Affad before he left and give it to him. However I didn't, and so I still have the letter. It is waiting for him, unless he wants me to send it on to Egypt; but he spoke vaguely of coming back soon so I put it in a safe place to await his arrival and . . ."

But suddenly at this juncture her blood ran cold, she put her hand to her cheek. Schwarz was saying, "But the old boy was in quite a bother, he seemed to think that you had either destroyed it in a fit of pique or that you had opened it yourself and knew the contents . . . what the devil is it, a love-letter?" He broke off as he saw the expression on her face. "Constance!" he cried sharply; and now she said, "Did you say Mnemidis had been at my bookshelf?" He spread wide his arms with an air of puzzled resignation. "But you gave him permission to borrow books, did you not?" She nodded, for she had in fact told him that he might have any book he wished to read, though her own shelves contained mostly text books and dictionaries and fat volumes of reference. She had really been thinking of the general clinic library which was not a bad little one, full of novels and general literature. "I *told* you he had carried off a lot of your books," said Schwarz somewhat irritably, "but he had your express permission." She nodded. She had missed the first allusion to the subject. "But the *Bible*," she said now, "the *Bible!* The letter of Affad I slipped into the Bible for safe-keeping!" She had gone quite pale and this puzzled him for he said, "Well, what about it? You can easily retrieve it. Mnemidis won't *eat* it after all, will he?" She hoped to goodness not; at the same time she was furious to think that all this fuss should be made over this petty question of a letter – though of course she knew (without really believing in them) what momentous issues hung upon its receipt. To know the hour of one's death – was it really so important? "You must ring up Pierre when he's on duty and tell him to retrieve it from the book. Mnemidis himself will be under full sedation for a while yet; he liked it so much that he asked for a second vacation from himself." He was perfectly right; Pierre would certainly secure the detested letter if he were asked. All this was quite true but so great was her anxiety and impatience that she slipped out into the lobby of the hotel and found a telephone. She rang the clinic and asked for the secretariat so that they could tell her the duty-hours of Pierre. Unfortunately he did not come on duty again until eight the following morning; the patient himself was in a sedation booth and his little room was locked up, so that it was idle to ask somebody else to hunt down the letter at such an hour. The best was to wait until Pierre came on deck again. For some reason or other she felt full of anxiety; she admitted to herself that there was really no reason to suppose that she would not recover the letter intact. Yes, but nevertheless... the whole matter rattled her in an obscure way.

She found the speeches stuffy and quite interminable and was glad when the evening came to an end and she was able to say goodnight to the glowing Schwarz and retrieve her car for the long drive back to the solitary lake house. She arrived late in a sort of remorseful triumph – a strange mood which shared the anxiety over the letter with the delightful sense of having advanced a pace in the direction of the child's good health. In both moods of course the thought of Affad echoed in her ears, so that she dreamed of him and woke somewhat disconsolate and disturbed.

The little alarm told her when to get her car and motor to the *auberge* to telephone to Pierre whose day watch began at eight in the morning. However, it took a moment to locate him and when she did he was at first quite startled and intrigued that she should ring so early. He listened to her with care and verified the fact of Mnemidis' borrowings; and, yes, among the books had been a Plato and a Spengler. But had been very specially glad of the little Bible, because (so he said) he had some things to confirm and verify. "C'est un drôle de coco celui-la!" confided the giant with a chuckle, but added that all the books were in the locker by his bed and would come to no harm. "Please," said Constance, "I want to ask you a favour – will you go and find the Bible? In it you should find a letter addressed to a M. Affad. It is from Egypt. If you can get hold of it I will come round and pick it up." He promised to go and have a look while she held the line. He was away for a considerable time, but this was not unusual for the high-security wing of the clinic had a bewildering number of sealed doors which one had to open first and then lock behind one.

But the letter was not in the book!

Nor was it any use repeating: "Are you sure? Are you absolutely *sure*?" Pierre felt the urgency in her tone and was correspondingly troubled. "I looked in all the books, and in the bundle of papers and folders. I also looked in his handbag to make sure it was not there. Then I went round the room, the shelves the shower cubicle, the . . . but everywhere, doctor, everywhere possible!" She closed her eyes and in her imagination photographed her consulting-room as well as the alcove with the built-in bookcase. Could it be perhaps that the letter had fallen out during the actual removal of the books? She telephoned to her secretary to ask if she had rescued any letter from the floor during her own absence, but the answer was in the negative. Where the devil had it got to? Had Mnemidis perhaps destroyed it, thrown it out into the wastepaper basket? Her heart sank at the thought of the complicated search which would have to be undertaken to verify such a hypothesis. She reproached herself for the exaggerated anxiety she felt about this trifling contretemps. Of course it would turn up, perhaps even Mnemidis when he woke might throw some light on the matter. It was best to wait calmly and let things take their course. This harangue to herself did little more than allay her native impatience for a brief spell. She looked at her watch. There would be time to verify matters for herself and still arrive (if she hurried) in time for the child's evening session which closed with dinner. She drove to her office and startled the somnolent Schwarz who was not used to late nights, and paid for them with several days of apathy and fatigue. "What's got into you?" he demanded plaintively; and she replied, "It's that bloody letter of Affad's. It has got mislaid. It has disappeared. It was in the Bible which Mnemidis took to study and which is now beside his bed covered apparently in jottings. I phoned Pierre to check. But no letter!"

With considerable exasperation she now went through her own consulting-room with a fine-tooth comb, so to speak, in the hope of tracing the article. In vain. Mnemidis had not after all taken so very many books: half a dozen in all. But of course the Bible had been among them.

She drove now up to the central clinic and the remote grey building which housed the dangerous cases, and just managed to catch Pierre as he was going off duty. Together they went upstairs, unlocking and locking a network of doors until they came to the little room where Mnemidis lived out the greater part of his strange life. The books were all there, and yielded nothing: nor did the patient's own papers, in the form of several folders containing letters and newspaper clippings. The bible was quite heavily marked up in pencil, as though he had read it with special attention. Perhaps for new impersonations? "And his handbag?" she asked. Pierre said, "It's with him. But I've been through it. Nothing!"

"Nothing!" she echoed with a sigh.

She sat down on the nearest chair and reflected deeply for an instant. The only hope left was perhaps that Mnemidis himself might provide a solution to the problem when it became possible to interrogate him – but that would not be for ten days as yet. She must possess her soul in patience until this last avenue could be explored. Perhaps he had inadvertently thrown it away or destoyed it: perhaps opened it? "Pierre," she said "I'm so sorry for the trouble I've given you. But the minute he comes round please help me interrogate him. He trusts you now, after that ridiculous episode with the egg!" The big "Malabar" smiled his slow saintly smile and nodded.

She calculated that there was just time to circle the town and visit her flat before returning to the château and her charge: she needed some clothes to wear in the little lake house by the water. While she was busy turning out a chest-of-drawers the phone rang. It was Sutcliffe, who was both surprised and delighted to catch her, though he sounded a trifle nettled that she had disappeared from circulation without leaving him a message. "Ah! There you are!" he said with a sort of testy joviality. "Perhaps you will favour me with some information as to where the devil you have gone to and why. Everybody is asking me. I have a right to know – or have I?" She explained that she had decided to deal with her fatigue by drastically reorganising her holiday-time – in fact she confessed where she was and what was afoot, though she swore him to secrecy. "That's the point," he said, "what do I tell the Prince? It's all about the fatal letter addressed to Affad. He is under the impression that you have taken destiny by the forelock and intervened."

"In what sense?"

"I mean simply carried off the letter with the intention of suppressing it or of losing it. I can just hear him saying to Affad, 'You see, the *moment* a woman interferes everything goes wrong.' So I implore you, for your own peace of mind and mine, to surrender that bloody letter to me and I will put it back in the bag and bang it off to Egypt."

"The letter has been mislaid!"

Sutcliffe whistled and fell silent. Then he said, "They won't believe you, you know."

"It's the truth," she said.

"I myself hardly believe you. Swear!"

"I swear! Cross my heart."

"They will think you have interfered with . . . well, with what they regard as Affad's destiny. I suppose you have been told about the letter, the death-signal, so to speak, and where it fits into their gnostic arrangements. O Lord!"

"Yes, I know what it means, though I take a rather poor view of all the mumbo-jumbo, and the secret society business. It's a very perverse and foolish philosophy."

"You are very pig-headed," he said angrily. "After all, the metaphysical problem is a real one. How to turn back the tide of spiritual entropy. The sacrifices are real, too. Affad is not alone, there is a man before and a man behind; he is part of a tradition which hopes to interrogate death itself. Now the old boy will certainly think you have made an unwarrantable intrusion into the affair. Probably that you have even opened the letter, or destroyed it. Do you know what is in the letter?"

"No. I swear!"

There was a long silence during which she could hear him whistling softly to himself—a sign of great perplexity and exasperation. "The whole thing is incredibly childish," she broke out, "and so Egyptian: why can't he get a copy of the message from the central committee or whatever? It is not the first time a letter has gone astray, been mislaid, is it?"

"Apparently he can't."

"Even the Prince?"

"So it would seem!"

With mounting irritation at all this portentous and childish behaviour she described the situation to him, adding that perhaps the problem would be solved when Mnemidis was woken from his artificial sleep. Sutcliffe sighed. "Well, I will do my best to put things in a favourable light, though I can foresee a good deal of scepticism about your own good intentions. They are bound to feel you are playing with them."

"If they do, then let me speak to them. I can quite easily convince them, I am sure."

But she was reluctant to push things further until this last avenue had been explored; suppose the madman had just hidden it somewhere – behind a radiator, say? Yes, but they had looked everywhere, specially in such places! "I've got to get back to my job," she said. "Schwarz is abreast of my movements and my work, if there is any untoward happening!"

It was puzzling that there was no news of Affad's return to Geneva: however, she did not wish to seem over-curious about the matter, and rang off, regained her car and set off for the château.

There was apparently nobody at home except the Swiss girl and she had to ring for a while before the door was opened; she was however radiant and smiling, though she put her finger to her lips and said, "Shh! He is having a nap. But my goodness, what a change! I hardly recognised him today. Constance, his eyes are open, he is looking, they have depth and being in them!" She clapped her hands, but noiselessly. Together they mounted the staircase and gained the elegant dressing-room which had been set aside for them, and where Constance divested herself of her coat and handbag while she listened to the report of the assistant therapist. "He did not weep for me – I'm afraid the whole transference thing is all yours! But the change was very marked, his whole face has opened up like a flower. And his smile! It's so new he hardly knows how to wear it. But don't listen to me; come and sit by him for a moment." Their silence was no longer necessary for the child was awake, gazing round him as he lay in his little bed, curling and uncurling his small hands as if he were about to employ them in doing something.

But no sooner did she lean down to kiss him and pick

him up than it started again, the weeping – but more slowly, more consciously. He was in the middle of a yawning fit, seized by a kind of fatigue; but he looked at her keenly, touching her hair and putting his finger almost in her mouth. And wept. As if it were the end of the world, the end of time. She took him up and cradled him once more, mentally encompassing his whole being with her circling arms. She felt that he had embarked upon the perilous attempt to forge for himself a human identity, and that the principal wound in the unconscious had been found if not identified. Would that he could weep his way back to articulate health! And today, as for some weeks to come, this cathartic weeping was the only fruitful dialogue which took place between them. But it also evolved, it did not remain static. There were days of anger and days of gloom; but very gradually, like the sun piercing clouds, elements of relaxation, almost of joy, manifested themselves. And these could be read upon his new face – one in which the eyes now played their full part, expressive, curious, sometimes almost roguish! Sometimes during his weeping he would let her put her finger softly on his nose, chin, forehead. But always he went the full length, crying until he was completely exhausted, worn out, hypotonic.

Gradually, too, as she advanced tiptoe into this uncharted territory, it seemed that she could "read" the infantile dilemma which had stunted the psychic growth of the child. What was also new was the feeling that now he was cooperating unconsciously with her. His muscle schemes were relaxing, he was drawing strength from her, and from the admission of his own weakness.

Some of the encounters sparked off other feelings, for example aggression; he would stab at her eyes with his fingers, or put them in her mouth with a rough intent, but which faded into helpless tears, as though the impetus had spent itself. In the aggression she read his reluctance to surrender to the soft appeals of reason and health. Then at other times the weeping ceased and he would lie in her lap for a spell, brooding as he listened to her singing. Sometimes he carefully touched her mouth again, and smeared his spittle round it carefully, as if following out some inner ritual. And sometimes also he might lie as calmly as a nursing infant making soft sounds with his voice, "*da da va va*". Once he put his mouth to her cheek in an involuntary gesture of affection, but was immediately seized by contrition and reverted to his blank, sightless look, turning his head away from her. But his eyes were at least open now, and he could now gaze even at the world outside the window of the playroom; or at the slowly unrolling lake scenery opening like a Japanese fan during the afternoon drive. The old grandmother reported that while he was still restless at night he had long periods when he was in a good mood, and his gestures and impulsive movements seemed less uncontrolled. The process would still be a long one, Constance felt, but the orientation had now changed in a more fruitful direction – the ship was on the right course. And with the first successes in this field she felt the whole weariness of her profession surge up in her. What was the point of effecting a psychic repair of this kind if one could not leave the patient to continue the work in competent hands? Who would replace her, who would communicate the loving care and the warmth to the little robot when she was forced to leave? For the moment the very evident success of the treatment was enough to keep her happy and enthusiastic, but already queries about the future rose in her mind; she had begun to divine what old age was all about! It would have been so good to spend the night with a man, instead of staying sealed off and frigid like this, incapable of warmth, of a simple, lustful response to life. This was the terrible weakness of setting too serious a valuation on experience. What to do? Once she had tried to break out of the prison of her sensibility by getting drunk at a cocktail party and succumbing to the charms of a pleasant younger colleague. But the episode had been like trying to ignite damp straw. She was humiliated not by his ineptness so much as her own inadequacy. How right Affad had been to insist so stoutly that all sex attachments are psychic and that the body is simply a reservoir of sensation. Loving from this point of view meant that reality was not compromised, and one faded into nature as if into a colour wash!

But if there was any fatuous disposition to self-congratulation over the increasing success of her treatment it was nipped in the bud by an incident, trivial in itself, which showed how intricate and strange are the associative schemes which provoke and underlie human behaviour. Or at least so it would seem from a remark made by the grandmother one afternoon as they drove slowly round the lake. The old lady who, for all her forbidding silences, was very observant, turned her large dark operatic eye on Constance and said, "You are not wearing the scent today!"

"It's probably because I went for a swim in the lake – but in fact I am, though it's much fainter. Do I smell of it so very much?"

The old lady smiled and shook her head. She said, "No, it's just that it is my daughter's scent, Lily's."

"You mean Jamais de la Vie?"

"Jamais de la Vie!"

Constance was dumbfounded, exasperated and professionally delighted – perhaps *this* is what had given her such an immediate associative transference with the child, had enabled her to penetrate his emotions so swiftly. And the tears . . . She went back over the old diagnoses in the light of this new gleam of knowledge. How lucky she had been, for her choice of a new scent to match a new hair-style, a new character change, had been quite haphazard. Had it in fact been a key? She turned to look at the small abstracted face beside her in the looming automobile and wondered. And if all human emotions and action depended on such an affective pattern of association-responses . . . It was a pure wilderness of associations, a labyrinth in which the sources of all impulse lay. Besides, it was after all sound psychology to trace the roots of emotion and desire to the sense of smell – its vast ramifications had never been completely worked out, and never would be. She tried to remember the smell of Affad – it was a sort of non-smell, like the smell of the desert: yet somehow at the heart of its airlessness there was a perfume, the odour of muscat or of cloves? (I hate literary emotions, she told herself!)

"I shall soon be leaving you," she said to the old lady, "as I must sooner or later return to my other cases. No, don't look alarmed! Not until I feel sure that everything is going well and that Esther can take over. Besides, I am always there if need be to consult. At the end of a phone!" This seemed to reassure the old lady and no more was said about the matter.

At the end of the excursion she carried the sleepy patient up the stairs to his playroom and set him down among toys which now were becoming objects of interest to him.

It was in the same week that another significant departure took place; the Swiss girl greeted her one day with a triumphant expression and said, "Eureka! Today he lifted the glass of milk himself and tried to feed himself. Constance, it's really marvellous!"

And Constance knew that she would soon be leaving; the obstinate Mnemidis had refused all knowledge of a letter in the bible, or indeed in any of the other books. It was quite baffling. Could he be lying, and if so why? And to make matters worse she at last received a letter from Affad, couched in the form of a reproach which she did not feel she merited. It made her feel furious, and also guilty. After all, in accepting the letter from Blanford she had had no clearly formulated plan – indeed, had she met Affad as she expected to do, she would have handed it over in the normal way. And here they were accusing her . . . It was really most vexatious and short-sighted.

> Dear Constance: I really did not think, my dear, that you would meddle in my affairs in such a resolute fashion; it is all too painful, and I understand your feeling that things can be prevented from happening by an act of resolution . . . But they can't. I regret having told you as much as I did about the structure of gnostic belief and the grave experiment our group is engaged in trying out. This stupid letter would have only contained a death-date, with no indication of how or by whom. That is the little bit of essential information which enables us to complete our *devoir*–without it we are just ordinary people, dispossessed, taken unawares: the original sin! It is the equivalent of letting me die unshriven! The knowledge of this simple fact enables one to take up a stance consciously towards the only basic feature of human existence which is never studied, is always avoided, is funked! People expire, they don't *die* in a positive sense, "mobilised in the light of nature"! I ask you to restore the letter to me. You have no right to it, and I have. I cannot believe that you would betray me like this even though you are a determinist, a behaviourist. Ah! What a stupid charge to lay against you! I am terribly sorry for such a sudden explosion of bad temper, but I am both frustrated for myself, my own *salut*, to use an ironic phrase, and also for the man or men after me. I am only a link in a long bicycle chain. I believe you understand this, as it is also expressed in sexual terms in our love for each other–has it *forever* vanished? Are you cured of me? Have you forgotten the beginning when we played cards by candlelight with the dying Dolores?

It came back to her now with a shock; no, she had not

really forgotten, she had just put aside the memory, perhaps out of pain, for Dolores had been her best friend at school and then later in medical school. When her husband who was a musician died she cut off her beautiful hair and threw it into the coffin. But it grew again, as beautiful as ever, and so did her only child. She was a brilliant surgeon among the younger ones, but by ill luck she infected herself and contracted a fatal type of poisoning. Constance used to take Affad to the ward at night to keep her company, and the three of them would play cards on the night table. As she grew weaker the effort increased but they kept up the habit out of friendship. One night the dying woman handed over her cosmetics and said that she would like to be sure that if she died suddenly in the night her face would be made up for her before her son was allowed in to see her. They promised, and set about playing the usual game of rummy. But tonight she felt much weaker, and kept fading away, drifting into quiet dozes; until with a small contrite shudder she simply stopped breathing. They were both shaken with sadness and resignation. Constance checked pulse and breath and then drew the lids down over the sad and dignified eyes. Affad put his arms round her and she embraced him with a triumphant abandon, touching his hair and throat and ears as if she were building up his image as a sculptor might from the moist clay of the primary wish for love; to affirm, to unite, to triumphantly rescue him from time. And later on when they went hand in hand down to the deserted buttery to make a cup of coffee, Affad had said, "As you know, when one has seen someone die, someone stop breathing, one realises with a start how one breath is hooked into another, is attached to another. In between the breaths is the space where we live, between the beforebreath and the afterbreath is a field or realm where time exists and then ceases to exist. Our impression of reality is woven by the breathing like a suit of chain mail. It is in that little space, between the breaths, in that tiny instant that we have started to expand the power of the orgasm, as a united synchronised experience, making it more and more conscious, mobilising its power and fecundity with every kiss. Constance, we can't go wrong. Love can't make any other sense now for us! God, how I wish I could make you pregnant in the light of this! She had replied, "If you go on talking like this, you will!" But he had not. Nor would he now. Well, it was something real and for her something new in orientation and intensity. Better than the usual business, making love in a sort of moral pigsty of vaguely good intentions. Or not at all. Or not at all.

> My whole time here has been taken up with silly discussions about this fatal letter; and I at first thought it was all a mistake. But now I am forced to conclude with the Prince that you took it upon yourself to execute a *coup de main* in my favour. Darling, it is most misguided. Please believe me when I tell you so. The Prince is also writing you, and has telephoned so many times that I feel quite ashamed. Constance . . .

She put down the letter thoughtfully and devoted a moment of reminiscence to that faraway period – how close it was in actual clock-time, and how far away in memory! They had lived out the attachment obsessionally – was the past tense correct? She listened, stiffened to attention, to her own heartbeats as if she interrogated them. Was Affad really *over*? In a paradoxical sort of way only he could answer such a question by the act of reappearing on the scene. They had worked not just for pleasure but for ecstasy, not for the merely adequate but for the sublime, and this is what seemed to her unique about their love. It was without sanctions, without measure, and wholly double. Nor could she envisage it being over because the experience had been so complete, had marked them both so irremediably! She swore slightly under her breath and tried to pretend that the whole thing had shown a regrettable weakness on her part, but she was being insincere and she knew it. And *now* the whole damned problem of the letter had come between them. It was with a resigned sadness that she packed up, locked the little lake house, and took the road back to the city.

Her flat seemed somewhat gloomy and forbidding, so she bustled about and dusted it and generally set things to rights. An empty frigidaire gleamed frostily at her, empty as the heart of a sun. Thence to the clinic where she found a gloomy and irate Schwarz waiting for her with a nasty gleam in his eye. "Listen," he said, "I have a bone to pick with you, about this Mnemidis caper. He has been restored to us safe and just as unsound of mind, though of course rested and ready for any mischief. Constance, we cannot go on with him, whatever you say; we are simply not equipped, even the high-security wing, to look after him as he must be looked after. He belongs to the civil law, and should be returned to the authorities. If you go on poking away at his paranoia you know full well what the result will be. There is no point in incurring senseless danger or difficulty. He is quite certainly beyond our help and I think we must admit it."

She sat down at her desk and said, "What about the letter?" Schwarz sighed and said, "No trace! Did you expect any? I didn't. He could have put it down the lavatory, of course." In a sudden burst of resolution she got up and took him by the shoulders. "I feel I must go on with him until I am sure that he did not see it; grant me a month or two more and I'll surrender him as you see fit. But I must try out the matter and see – for Affad's sake."

"For Affad's sake," he echoed despondently. He swivelled his office chair round and pushed his spectacles back on his head. "Another thing! What do we do about visitors? Several people have asked to see him, including a doctor from

Alexandria who claims to have had him both as a friend and also under his wing. Now a *prison* has its security rules and all its precautions. A prison could answer these people. But we have no code of rules. Do we let *anyone* in who wishes to see him? One is a doctor, one a business associate . . ." He was in a frightful temper, she could see that. But, to be truthful, the problem was a relatively new one. "Could we not establish a visiting day like the state prison?" He said, reminding her, "what do you mean by 'close detention'? Define it."

They sat glumly staring at each other for a long moment. She knew that in this mood he would not give in unless she wheedled. It was unfair, but . . . "Please help me," she said. "I feel I am only doing my duty in making sure. It's the least I can do. And after that I promise to be good, *absolutely* good!"

So they came to a compromise about the treatment as well as the visitors, and she won her way over the misgivings of the sighing Schwarz.

But of the letter there was no sign; yet Mnemidis' way of talking about it, of answering questions about it, seemed somehow sly. He talked sideways, turning his face away, and said, "From who to who, and why? What a strange name, from Egypt certainly? Yes, from Egypt originally perhaps. Why should I have seen it? The Bible? It is full of untruths. And there are no *dates* so you cannot tell when it all happens!" In the middle of all this verbiage she imagined an occasional gleam, the barest hint which suggested that perhaps . . . But she was also aware of the desire which might lead her into a self-deception. The long sleep had done him good in a way for he was much fresher and his ideas flowed more freely. But of course what was missing was the basic connecting links between them – it was the standard paranoid configuration. And of course she was on the lookout for the first signs of persecution-delusions which pointed to danger for the therapist. Persecution was the code sign of violence, and she must be careful not to provoke this vein of feeling by too great insistence in her questions.

He had been watching the nuns from his window, for among the nurses on the wards there were a number of young nuns. He was intrigued to hear that they belonged to a silent order – he who spoke so much, in torrents, indiscriminately! "When there is nobody there I can still hear myself talking to myself, it still seems necessary – my whole intellectual formation and my expensive education all led to this state of affairs. I wish I could see some end to this situation because sometimes I am out of breath and out of voice. I get headaches even. But on goes the torture of the dialectic – the parallel straight lines which are supposed to meet at infinity, but never do. I know this because I have reached infinity, I am there, and still they haven't met." His eyes filled with tears, beautiful violent eyes which had only known one kind of rapture – death! The clock chimed, it was the end of the new session. She told him that arrangements had been made for him to see his friend the doctor on the morrow, and Mnemidis nodded, smiling enigmatically, joining his hands on his midriff like a mandarin. But the name stirred no particular echo. As for the letter, it appeared to have vanished for good. Was it worth being obstinate and keeping on?

It was at this juncture that Lord Galen, like some long-forgotten carnival figure, strayed on to the stage, so unexpected a presence that for a moment she could not fit his name into her memory. "My dear Constance," he said reproachfully, "of all people to forget *me*. Of all people!" She expressed an unfeigned contrition for she loved old Lord Galen – the mention of his name made one want to smile. And here he was, vague and wide-eyed as ever, with his rolled copy of the *Financial Times* under his arm. He carried it about as others might carry about a book of poems or a novel, to be dipped into during the day. They had lunch at a fashionable place and he signed the cheque with a flourish in the name of some international agency. In answer to her query he said, "My dear, I have come here to coordinate things. After a big war there is a lot of coordination necessary. They have made me Coordinator General of the Central Office of Coordination. I oversee almost everything and in a twinkling coordinate it! It is an immense saving of time and money for us all." She was tempted to ask him what his salary was, but refrained. He also apparently lectured, on the subject of which he obviously had a perfect command. But just what it *was* she never found out. He had learned it in America, he said. "I am very *pleased* with America!" he said, as if awarding a school prize. "After those beastly Germans it is just fine to be a Jew in America. America speaks with a Jewish voice and that goes for a lot. After all we won the war and now we will win the peace. Constance, you are smiling! Have I said something *effulgent*? I have come here to coordinate World Jewry. It may take a moment, and I may have to make sacrifices, perhaps take a cut in my *frais de représentation*. But what of it? And by the way I have managed to get Aubrey a decoration for his bravery–an O.B.E. You should have seen his face when I told him! He was pale with pride and surprise. He never expected his gallantry to be recognised but I saw to it. One word to the Prime Minister and . . ."

Aubrey's own version of these events, when she mentioned all this, was characteristically different, for the whole episode bordered on the grotesque and filled him with moroseness. "As for being pale with pride I was white to the gums with humiliation. Imagine! One day without warning the door of my room is thrown open by the obsequious Cade and a group of pin-striped notables is ushered in. It includes the consul-general and two consular clerks, Sutcliffe, Toby, Lord Galen and two other gentlemen who were described as journalists. You can imagine my alarm as they converged on me. I thought they had come to castrate me perhaps. The consul, Nevinson, held a Bible and a casket while the consular clerk held (for reasons best known to himself) a large parchment citation and a lighted candle. My hypothesis changed – they had obviously come to excommunicate me. Lord Galen then made an artless speech of fascinating inaccuracy and unconscious condescension. He praised everything except my physical beauty – my civic sense, my unflinching bravery under enemy fire, my example, my long suffering, *mon cul* – everything! I lay there between the sheets like a stale sandwich and allowed all this to pour over me. It was all the more humiliating as among them was Sutcliffe's boss Ryder whose wife had almost been buried alive in a London bombardment; she had lost a hand and an eye, while here was I . . . You can imagine. Then the consul cleared his throat and read out a long and incoherent citation written in a style which suggested that it had been swiftly run up that morning by someone on the *Daily Mirror*. Then he pinned a decoration to my pyjamas and a champagne cork popped in true ceremonial fashion. I nearly cried with rage. Then to round off everything Lord Galen imparted to us all his philosophy of life which went like this: 'The moment has come to invest in bricks and mortar. You can't go wrong if you do.' And Toby, who had just been to a Geneva bank to cash a cheque said, 'Have you noticed? The peculiarly tender way that bankers take each other by the shoulders and gaze into each other's eyes, as if they were caressing each other's fortunes which equalled their private parts?' Lord Galen hadn't, and he became somewhat huffy."

Constance cocked a professional ear to this unwonted vivacity of discourse and felt that things were very much better for Aubrey, that he was really on the mend. He could already just about stand up on his two feet and there were plans afoot for him to take a few steps during the following week. The operations had been strikingly successful. And this sudden improvement in health had encouraged him once more to think of his book, the "authorised version" of which still lingered among the disordered papers of Sutcliffe, the incorrigible and depraved shadow which hung over his life. "By the way, Affad rang up," he said a little maliciously and watched her carefully to see what the effect on her composure was. But she replied to him coolly and gave him an account of the contretemps about the letter, and about her battle of wits with Mnemidis. He sighed and shook his head. "He will be coming back anyway," he said, "though he didn't say when. By the way, talking of scandal, I discovered something quite extraordinary. Lord Galen has been frequenting the *maisons de tolérance* of the city, and in one of them he ran into Cade, who has suddenly started to take an interest in the low life. It would seem that Lord Galen is having trouble with his erection and that his doctors in London despaired of securing the right stimulus for him. So after trying everything without avail they suggested the Continent as a probable place where such matters are taken more seriously. Moreover in Geneva there is a special bankers' brothel called *le Croc* which specialises in such troubles and here Cade has found a billet also."

"I wonder what he is up to? Have you asked him?"

"Yes. He scratches his head and ponders a long time before replying in that dreadful Cockney whine, 'It makes a nice change.' In his pronunciation nice is naise and change chinge. My God, Constance, with all this talk about me I completely forgot to tell you how beautiful you look – the new style is unhingeing. Kiss me, please, to show you still care – *will* you?" This gallantry was also something new, though there was no lack of warmth in her embrace; he knew how much she loved him, and that he could ask anything of her. What better therapy, he asked himself, than this? "And even a new perfume to set off the graces of the new woman! Bravo!" He knew she was trying to outface the loss of Affad, to pick herself up off the ground, so to speak. But it had to be said in all friendship, lest she suspect him of "tactful" silences.

"Did Affad say when?"

"He said soon, very soon."

"*Eh bien*," she said, trying to sound indifferent, resigned.

But in fact the resumption of her city rhythm was a welcome thing; she had decided to visit the child less regularly and hope for a transfer of trust and affection to the real nurse, the Swiss girl. She had taken the precaution of leaving her a bottle of Lily's perfume to help things along. But here in the middle morning she was able to meet and question Aubrey's surgeons about his condition and inevitably Felix Chatto dropped in for a glass, together with Toby and the hangdog *patibulaire* Sutcliffe, looking as much a gallows' bird as ever. But how happy they all seemed to see her again! And how happy she was to rejoin them once more.

That afternoon Schwarz brought the alienist from Alexandria to meet her and discuss the case of Mnemidis. He apparently wished for a brief clinical discussion before embarking on the interview with his ex-patient and one-time friend. He was a tall lean man with a rasping voice like a crow. Impeccably dressed and hatted with a dark Homburg. He carried a stick with a golden knob which gave him a slight touch of sorcerer-on-holiday. His spatulate hands ended in long filbert nails, well tended. His face was pale, long, goat-like, with sulphurous yellowish eyes, a bit bloodshot as if from alcohol. But he had a kindly if commanding presence, and he called Mnemidis "our friend" with a conspiratorial smile, and formally alluded to Constance once as "my dear colleague" which showed the quality of his manners. He had apparently brought a letter for Mnemidis, and he was hoping to spend ten minutes with him – this had already been accorded. "But I wanted first of all to tell you that I have really come to negotiate his release under guarantee. His sponsor is an ex-associate, a millionaire from Egypt who will offer you every guarantee as far as security and safety is concerned in the question of actually transporting him back to his native land. I would only like to know the actual legal matters to be adjusted: what forms must I fill in, what permissions obtain?" They talked round the subject in a desultory way at first; Constance thought that the authorities would be glad to relinquish him under caution, and be rid of him. But they would have to examine the legalities involving criminal law. "That is precisely what his associate is doing today. I expect to be word-perfect this evening and tomorrow we can start a release-plan."

"That is rather quick work."

"Well, we can be patient if necessary. Geneva is a most interesting town where we have many friends. I wonder, doctor, if you would consider dining with me tonight? I would be honoured."

She hesitated, but finally agreed; the goat-like emissary might know Affad! He might have some information. She cursed herself inwardly as she heard her own voice say, "Thank you, doctor, that would be a great pleasure." He rose to his full height and with an awkward angular gesture put out his hand to shake hers. She felt obscurely that he had been looking and talking to her as if to a person about whom he had heard a lot. But perhaps this was just another self-delusion, unworthy of such an exalted personage as a psychologist! Nevertheless she would go! Nevertheless!

He was already seated at a corner table by the time she entered the old Bavaria, with its pseudo-Austrian furnishings and sedate walls covered with framed political cartoons. He explained that he had come early to secure a corner table, having read in the paper that a great international conference was opening that day, and knowing of old how congested both hotels and restaurants became during such events. He was very much in *tenue de ville* and wore a dark stock with pearl-headed pin which made him seem like a barrister or judge. It was only after a while that she realised that he was passably tipsy which gave his discourse great smoothness; he had lost his raven's croak.

"Did you have your interview?" she asked and he said that he had had a rather unsatisfactory meeting with Mnemidis. "He is very distraught by the questions the doctors keep putting to him. He confuses them with the police. You see, he has always been in a privileged position in Egypt; you probably don't know, but he has the gift of healing among his other less pleasant attributes. He is famous and has made a fortune for his Cairo associate Ibrahim. So occasionally when he does escape and spends a few days in the *souks* of Cairo with the inevitable result, a blind eye is turned to the matter, though of course they sweep him up and imprison him again. He had the luck once to cure the chief of police of a stone, a gall-stone. After being touched by him Memlik Pascha passed the stone without difficulty, thus avoiding the operation we had all said would be necessary. As you know, Egypt is a strange, superstitious sort of place. They see the world in a different way. It is hard for us Greeks or Jews of the second capital, Alexandria, because we are for the most part brought up in Europe, and we see things with your eyes. But we also see their way. A split-vision. Of course a lot has to do with simple definitions. In Mnemidis *you* see a subject with a florid paranoia and an epileptoid inheritance resulting in bouts of acute hypomania and so on: but last night Ibrahim was telling me that he was born in the sign of the Ram; with Mars and Sun in opposition in Pluto; his moon mal-aspected in Scorpio, a magnetic dissonance between the Lion and Mercury in the eighth house . . . It depends where you want to look for an explanation of the formidable double-bind which triggers him off." He turned his thirsty yellow eyes on her with a benign smiling weariness and rubbed his hands, as if he had just demonstrated something with them. She had begun to like him, for on the underside of his conversation, which was so assured, she felt a diffidence and a shyness which was most appealing. She longed to ask him if he knew Affad – after all she had accepted the evening invitation to do just that – yet her cursed pride held her bound to her reserve. What was to be done with a woman like herself?

"I suppose it is a different reality," she said, and he replied, "Very different but not less plausible once you realise how tricky words are! Our so-called scientific reality is a mere presumption suitable for certain intellectual exercises; but we dare not believe in it, completely, wholeheartedly. We cannot swear that the electron has no sex-life . . . but I am being silly! Thank you for smiling! But where the hypothesis of the individual ego with 'its' soul rules, as in a Christian state, people live in a state of unconscious hallucination. Is that too strong?"

"No. The problem has entered psychiatry."

"I don't think you are right, doctor. Or else we are talking at cross-purposes. The Freudian system at any rate works through and *with* the hypothesis of an individual ego."

"And Jung?"

"The doctrine has begun to crumble in Jung who is a Neo-Platonist in temperament. In that sense you are right. But all the discoveries are from Freud, he has all the honours. If the thing doesn't work 100 per cent, why, it is not his fault. He will become out of date just as Newton has. But for *us*, for *now*, we can't do without his genius."

"And Mnemidis, when he gets back to Egypt, will he be free to assume his old life? I mean will he be allowed his forays?"

"I expect he will be under reasonable surveillance – who knows? The police may turn him into an instrument, directing his activities: Memlik is quite capable of that. But nobody cares, any more than you care if a sportsman bags a couple of rabbits before lunch one day. In India, where everything began, this kind of human activity, obscene in itself, was undertaken on behalf of a goddess, called, I think, Kali; the murder was an act of so-called *thugee*, I was told."

"Good Lord!"

"An appropriate exclamation," he said, pouring himself out more wine. "In Cairo there is so much confusion, noise, lights, dust, fleas, people, daylight and darkness that nobody who disappears is really missed. I myself, when I was in my professional-doctor mood, tried a thing or two on our friend out of curiosity. He had a paranoid delusion that the walls of his room were closing in on him. Well, I had a detention cell specially made for him in which the walls really did close at the rate of five inches a day. You know, he reacted positively when it became obvious that it was not a delusion, it was true: the walls *were* closing in! One is at home in one's delusions and only asks to have them verified."

"Yes, I am aware of all the dialectical clevernesses, but they do little to help us find a therapy. Discussions about reality belong in the domain of the philosopher, and one presupposes *him* to be sane – another question mark! Are *you* happy about Mnemidis' activities?"

"No. For my part I would have him put away. I go even further: I think a healthy society would have him put away, after having tried to cure him for some years. Detention is no use."

"But?"

"But I may be wrong. The constitution of things may be juster than I am capable of supposing. Besides, look at the mess which comes about when I decided to take things into my own hands and act – Hitler! What an illustration of the misuse of the will, what misuse of human endeavour! And what is the use of getting rid of the poor Jews if you keep monotheism? It's crazy thinking."

"You should talk to Schwarz."

"I have. He agrees with me."

"Are you a Jew?"

"Of course. Everyone is a Jew!"

He had started to sound a trifle indistinct, as if the drink were beginning to tell on him; but he read her mind and said, reassuringly, "I sound drunk, don't I? I am not really. I took an overdose of a sleeping-draught yesterday by accident and the result is that I can hardly keep awake today. Excuse me."

"Should you drink?"

"Perhaps not; but after I have seen you home I am proposing to visit an old friend for a nightcap, and I must be in good form for him. Perhaps you know Sutcliffe?"

"Of course! Do you know him?"

"I have always known him. We are old hands, so to speak. I have been out of touch with him for a fairish time and am anxious to compare notes with the rogue."

"And Blanford?"

"I only know of him through Sutcliffe himself–something about collaboration on a book which wasn't going too well; according to him each one was trying to drag the sheets over to his side of the bed, and the book was suffering from it. I gather Sutcliffe has some sort of job here which he hates. As for 'our friend' Mnemidis he will be happy to get back home to Cairo. His nerves are at breaking-point under the questioning, so he says. Speaking in Arabic of course; he says you are putting a truth-drug in his food so he refuses it with the result that he is always hungry."

"O God!" she said with dismay. ". . . It's started!"

"I thought you must know, he must have said something."

"No. I was waiting for it, however! O what a dismal business it is when the persecution thing rears up. It's unfair!"

He laughed and said, "Yes: all is silent save for the noise

of swearing psychoanalysts getting the locks on their doors changed! Are you in the telephone book?"

"Yes. But I think we can ignore the graver eventualities in this case. Swiss detention is severe and exact. Still!"

"As you say, 'Still!'"

"Should I break off the interviews now before he turns nasty? Of course he himself may refuse to continue; and I was so much hoping... However, I will tell Schwarz that the milk has turned – the expression is his."

"I should personally break it off."

It was a depressing thought to feel forced to conclude this promising line of enquiry – she could see the phantom letter slowly dissolving as a reality. Tomorrow she would recover her Bible and say goodbye to this striking madman on whom all pity and sympathy would be lost because he seemed to be completely filling a destined role, something for which he had been born. In murder he perfected himself, you might say! An existentialist formulation worthy of the Left Bank! Where the Jewish Babel was being built by Sartre and Lacan and their followers, swarming like flies on the eyeballs of a dying horse! She had had many a disagreement about this with Affad whose fatal indulgence for letters often made him excuse any sort of dog-rhetoric, or so she told him. And here they had come to the end of the evening and the fatal mental block against mentioning his name was as fast as ever. She sighed, and her companion smiled and said, "I expect you are sleepy. In Geneva one does not siesta as in my country, so that one makes a poor showing in the evening if one stays late."

"I am sorry."

"It was not a reproach."

He walked her back to her flat along the tranquil park-fringed borders of the lake, talking quietly about their patient, and about his plans for transplanting him, as he put it, back to the sumptuous apartment among the mosques which had been his before the present imbroglio had altered the balance of things. In the course of the coming week the legal side of the question would be settled, and then they would be free to devise the safe transfer of the patient. "Doubtless *you* will miss him and be full of a professional regret; but he is easily replaced, when you think of it. Almost any prime minister of any European country . . . As for him he spends hours at the little window of his new room which overlooks the kitchens. He is lost in admiration for the nuns."

"I didn't know."

"Yes. There is a silent order of nuns who are in charge of a whole wing and who do much of the catering for the whole establishment. The kitchens have big bay-windows and he can see them moving about preparing the food for the inmates, like 'feluccas' (I am quoting) for they wear those tall starched white coifs on their heads and broad white collars over their black vestments. I spent a while with him watching them, for I offered to go back with him and Pierre very kindly let me. They are very striking, they look like Easter lilies to me, the shape of the coif, and our friend wondered whether they were really silent by choice or whether they had become dumb owing to the lies disseminated in the Bible which he is reading so avidly. But he is so sane that he remains very cunning and one can't tell if he is lying or not–because he does not himself know. What a predicament to be in! Maybe it is what overturned the reason of men like Nietzsche. I have often wondered." It seemed rather a strange proposition, so she did not attempt to embroider on it. But in general how strange the preoccupations of lunatics were; what could Mnemidis find in the view of the nuns in the kitchen?

But everything has its answer. The blue unmediating infant's gaze of Mnemidis fixed itself, not upon the nuns in their picturesque uniforms, but upon the two great carving knives with which they so expertly cut up the daily bread of the establishment before distributing it deftly among the yellow baskets. He sighed when the operation was at an end and the baskets were loaded on to trays and trolleys and carried away to the refectory; he sighed as if woken from a dream of some total abstraction which had held him spellbound. This was indeed the case. His whole day orientated itself upon the appearance, as if upon a stage, of the nuns. The kitchens blazed suddenly with white light. A van drove up to the door, the back opened; the drivers lifted out a number of tall baskets with the loaves of bread in them. Into the kitchen they went and the nuns, seizing the two flashing, sabre-like products of the Upinal Steel Federation (often given away as pure advertisements) began their absorbed Christian sacrifice, cutting up the body of Christ into eatable-sized slices. In this way the Word would be made flesh at last; as for the wine, the blood, that would come later. Meanwhile the knives rose and fell, flashing in the sunlight, or poked and thrust with peristaltic suggestibility until with one hand he found himself fingering his private parts and deeply thinking. Deeply, passively thinking. Happiness lies in this sort of concentration, this surrender to one's inmost nature. What could be more innocent than a loaf of bread? It hardly felt the knife enter it, purr through its white flesh. The Upinals were terribly sharp always, they were known by the excellence of their superior steel. What better steel for a sacrificial knife, then? Mnemidis watched humbly, taking in every detail. Sometimes he broke off and made a short circle around the writing table, only to come back once more to the window and concentrate on this gripping vision of the nuns cutting up their Saviour. Give us this day . . .

Of some of this matter Constance was aware, but not of all; but the news that Mnemidis was running short of patience and simmering into revolt was depressing in the extreme. Though she had been tired at the dinner-table and was glad that her host walked her back to her flat relatively early, she found that sleep evaded her. Nor did a sleeping draught help matters, so she read a little, and then rose to make coffee for herself – a fatal decision. A profound depression seized her, and about everything – her life, her work, her profession, her future . . . It was like sliding down a bank of loose sand into a deep pit of self-reproach and, which was worse, self-pity. It would not do. She played a game of solitaire on the green card-table and after a while felt the drug beginning to work on her nerves. Sleep became once more a possible achievement, however troubled, so she risked getting back into bed with her book. On an impulse she did what she did quite often, picked up the telephone and dialled the time-clock. The announcer's recorded voice was not unlike Affad's, though the accent was different. She allowed him to recite the passing of time for about two whole minutes before shame drove her to cut him off. But her self-reproach became actualised by the dream voice of Max as he guided her through the *asanas*, forcing her to take them slowly, and at each stage to pin-point the nothingness-quotient of her mind, half narcotised now by the drug. It was clumsy, lop-sided yoga and would have merited a rebuke from the old man, but it had the desired effect for it shifted her attention from herself – sleeplessness is in the first instance simply exaggerated self-importance – and allowed her to lower herself into the warm pit of night with a mind too tired to manufacture any more dreams. No more dreams!

She slept.

FOUR

The Escape Clause

IT HAD BEEN STIRRING WITHIN HIM NOW FOR DAYS, AND HE was aware of a gradually growing constraint in his feelings about the outer world – first towards his keeper Pierre and then the doctor, that handsome woman who made everything sound glib and roguish. He knew now that everything she had been telling him was false, and came from the Black Bible she had loaned him. Her smile, moreover, was false as a mouse-trap – *une souricière de sourire !* First she had thrust him down into full oblivion with her medicines: now it was this mysterious letter. He had perused it negligently, vaguely noting the date it contained, and that not precise. It said "*à partir de . . .*" which seemed to offer no very exact information. Nor had this anything to do with his own concerns – the gradually overwhelming, suffocating, feeling which would evolve slowly into the basic cold hate upon which his actions would be based. Hush! she must not become aware of his state of mind, he must pretend to be pious, for they were all Christians and had been brought up in a vengeful code, always seeking moral redress, always thinking sacrificially. For some time now when he heard Pierre's footsteps on the gravel he would hasten to kneel down and feign to be deep in prayer when the Judas clicked open. No doubt this was reported. He watched her reactions carefully when he criticised the good book; he intended at the very end suddenly to pretend that he had been converted, that after all he had come to believe in it. That would put her off her guard and make her become perhaps more negligent in her habits. He had already reflected on how much energy it would need to overpower Pierre in the course of their walk across the wood. It is true that the negro was built like a house, but that did not seem to Mnemidis an over-riding consideration. He was agile and versed in the ju-jitsu style of wrestling. And he was totally unafraid, his wholehearted self-dedication gave him the strength of a lion. He felt the current of his desire sweeping through his body like a stream of electricity. There was only one question which created a difficulty in his planning. *L'arme blanche*, in the expressive French phrase – the crucial *knife* which he needed for his self-expression. At home in Cairo he had a wall collection of them – beautiful knives of all calibres with which he practised assiduously. He could both throw and stab at will, and as suddenly as a snake striking. No real problem here. It was only the details which remained to be worked out.

The mention of Cairo now, that was a new factor in his thinking, a new promise of life and freedom. The whole matter had filled him with renewed enthusiasm for his avocation. To quit this dull grey Swiss background for the brilliant Cairo of his youth – goodness, his heart sang within him! And just as a farewell present he would, as a *pourboire*, so to speak, leave them a knife-print or two in his best vein before leaving. It would be his going-away present for the sterile world of doctors and priests and policemen. Who did they think he was? *He was, after all, Mnemidis, the one and only member of his species.* Old B., the doctor, used to tease him about this proposition, but really it was the truth. B. used to joke and say, "Now tell me to which species do you belong? Imaginary Man, Marginal Man, Fortuitous Man, Superfluous Man, Parallel Man? . . ." And he would reply, "To none, to none. I am the incarnation of Primal Man. I am perfected in my sainthood because I know not the meaning of Fear!" As he spoke he had a sudden vision of his own consciousness hanging in the air above him – brilliantly iridescent and glowing, a self-perfected globe of celestial light, throbbing and hovering in an atmosphere of pure bliss of which he was the human instrument. He was the pure spirit of the perfected Act! It had all come to him from that first day when as an adolescent he had strangled the little Bedouin child who had come to the house to beg for work. So silently, his lust glowing like a great ruby in his mind. In this way he had separated himself from the rest of humanity.

Yes, the thought of Cairo struck a new note, and the sudden arrival upon the scene of ancient associates with their promise of freedom excited him unduly. Moreover when they spoke to him in Arabic, as the doctor did, he felt quite disarmed, and incapable of keeping a secret about his feelings, about his eagerness to be done with the Swiss scene. But the doctor urged compliance upon him, and patience and watchfulness; a hasty move might spoil his chances of an escape. There were documents to be filled in, people to be consulted. Nevertheless he felt in honour bound to make it clear that since he realised that he was being systematically poisoned he found it much harder to set aside his feelings of impatience and frustration. Much, much harder.

Nor could he help noticing that his jailors had redoubled their precautions, for his person, his cell and his meagre possessions were subjected every morning to the most careful scrutiny by Pierre who dwelt lingeringly upon each object, as if he were trying to memorise it, humming softly as he did so. What charm the man had! Mnemidis ground his teeth soundlessly, feeling the muscles at his temples contract and relax. He had a secret premonition that it would not be long now, things were moving into the sort of spiral which quickened into the catharsis of action.

His intuitions seemed verified almost at once, for on presenting himself for the usual interview he was confronted by the surly figure of Schwarz who informed him that the long treatment was to be discontinued. "I understand you have expressed strong reservations about the doctor treating you, and in deference to them I have had her transferred to another field of enquiry. On her return from leave she will undertake other duties. I hope this will satisfy your sense of justice." This sounded a most elaborate and juicy climb-down, and the patient was all smiles at his unexpected victory; he rubbed his hands and bowed. Then his face darkened again with a renewed wave of doubt, for it seemed to him that they were trying to shirk their responsibilities; after all, the damage had been done. The poison was already permeating his whole system, and now they were talking of abandoning him. No, it wouldn't do, it wouldn't do at all! "It's all very well," he said at last, with a smouldering glance of contempt, "but what about all I have been through, all the questions, the waste of time . . . eh?" Schwarz sighed and said patiently, "I hope you will soon forget your ordeal. Tomorrow or the next day you will be returned to the civil authorities and they will arrange for you to join your two friends and return to your homeland. Surely that must please you?" Mnemidis moistened his lips and asked if it were true. "Of course it is true," said Schwarz, who now permitted himself the faintest tinge of joviality. And indeed his two friends, as if to prove the correctness of the doctor's announcement, presented themselves with good news. The transfer was being negotiated, there was no impediment in law, and within a week or ten days they would present themselves with all the papers and a special Red Cross ambulance to take him to the airport where a special plane would be waiting, bound for Cairo. It was like a dream, he wept as he thought of it, but sadly, for it had come too late. They would not avoid their retribution quite so easily, particularly the woman. The whole thing had been her idea, the whole cunning interrogatory had been devised by her with the idea of making him doubt himself. That night he wet his bed. He was assailed with extraordinary dreams and visions of power and omnipotence; he became once more the child divinity whose purpose burned within him like a lamp of grace. His tongue swelled up in his mouth like a puff adder, then his whole throat. He woke late but ready for anything. He had a feeling the hour was at hand, though for the moment the details were not clear; they would come.

When there is such a stylist in mischief as Mnemidis prepared for action, the very spirit of mischief presents itself in order to facilitate things. In this case it was the Swiss mania for insignificant detail which played the part. Before parting with their visitor it was essential that the documentation upon his case be complete; hence the long and exhausting series of blood-tests and nerve-tests, of analyses and readings, of cephalograms and cardiograms . . . the whole rigmarole of quantitative science must have a final outing before restoring him to his world of occasional involuntary murder. He had to blow into tubes, swallow liquids, stand on one leg, kneel and lift weights. He waited patiently and most obediently throughout all this, waited for the door which he knew would open. He went from laboratory to laboratory like a lamb, watched over by Pierre, whom he had come to love like a brother. But he was in a state of heightened attention, he noticed every lock, bolt and bar; yet for the time being nothing beckoned him, nothing whispered conspiratorially in his ear to say, "Now! This is it!" And apart from all this the change and the movement were refreshing for someone suffering from over-confinement.

The last of these investigations were the most elementary, and usually took place first, on entry into the hospital. There was a tank-like changing room with seats and lockers on all sides, changing-screens and douches. In here were machines which recorded your height and weight and such vital facts as general corpulence or the circumference of calves and breasts. The entry corridor to the whole complex contained notice-boards and toilets, and finally opened into the spacious dining-rooms and kitchens. It was in this tank-like precinct that the magical whisper came and communicated itself to Mnemedis.

To divest himself of the long-sleeved regulation coat of pleasant green tweed and his woollen vest he stepped behind a screen while Pierre, respecting the delicacy of one who had been "born a gentleman", did not follow him but stood and waited on the other side; the articles of clothing were thrown upon the screen and Mnemidis, stripped now to the waist, looked strangely coy and playful. Ignoring the weighing machine which stood waiting for him, he gave his jailor a sudden push with both hands, catching him off his guard, and with one and the same movement, propelled himself through the door and into the corridor where he promptly turned the key upon Pierre and went off–but slowly, thoughtfully, for he knew that if one moves slowly people suspect nothing–and entered the network of locker-rooms and privies which led to the kitchens. One cannot describe him as thinking all this out in detail; he was really sleepwalking, letting instinct guide him. Flashes of light like a summer lightning dazzled him from time to time and he blinked his eyes. He heard the voice of Pierre and the rattling of the door but was not alarmed at all. A wild certainty possessed him. The spirit of mischief was in the saddle. He went solemnly and industriously from room to room, locking each door behind him, and so at last came to the spacious kitchens which were empty. He stopped to gaze about him, noted with appreciation the warm sunlight shining through the high windows upon the spotless array of cooking utensils lining the walls. It was very Swiss in its impeccable cleanliness, the great kitchen, one felt that no germ would find a harbour there; it smelt clinical and pure, its air filtered by the clean flowing draught of fans. But he was looking for something and had no time to waste on idle appreciation of his surroundings. From his window on the opposite side of the court his gaze fell . . . just where? He made a swift calculation and changed direction. Yes, the bread-bins and the wall of tins was on the right, surely they must be there? There!

The knives, spotless as the rest, were there!

With the current of joy and affirmation flowing through his body he contemplated, giving thanks to his creator; he even joined his hands before his breast and shook them in thanksgiving, like a Christian. Then with a sneaking, smiling air of happiness, he took up first one and then the other of the knives and felt its exquisite balance in the palm of his hand; it was as pregnant with futurity as an egg. At this moment the swing-doors at the end of the kitchen opened and in swayed the monumental form of Pierre, looking puzzled, for this had never happened to him before and he found it surprising. Moreover with Mnemidis now stripped there was no sleeve to grab in order to tame and pivot him. The big man was suddenly realising that much of his mastery over things, over people, was due to familiar routines; the lack of that basic sleeve troubled and disoriented him. Nor had he seen Mnemidis ever look quite like this – blithe and exuberant, his whole bearing suffused with a glory from on high. He proposed to play cat and mouse with Pierre, but jovially, with kindliness, for he really loved and esteemed this companion of his solitary hours. He put the hand with the knife behind his back and beckoned Pierre to approach with the other, playfully, teasingly; and when the "Malabar" obeyed he dodged back and round, in and out among the sinks and cupboards. They performed a slow and somewhat elaborate ballet in this way, passing across the great kitchens in a sort of gruesome two-step for Pierre was fully aware of the knife and of the danger he was in from a sudden change of mood. It would have been wise for him to pick a weapon for himself and try to despatch the madman with a lucky blow on the head – a saucepan, perhaps: but he preferred to be patient and not provoke a flare-up of aggressiveness. He was calm and confident of the outcome and only concerned lest he might obtain a wound while trying to disarm Mnemidis. Moreover, dancing about like this they were killing time and it could not be long before somebody came into the kitchens and then Pierre could shout for help in surrounding his man. Where were the sisters? Where was the staff of the place? There was no sign of a soul. They continued on their appointed courses like two ill-omened planets in orbit – planets engaged in a gravitational flirtation which could only end one way, in a collision!

Neither was the least out of breath as yet, and watching the intense concentration with which they danced an observer might have thought their synchronised and stylised motion the result of long rehearsal. But there was method in Mnemidis' madness – to coin a phrase; he had seen a half-open door which gave on to a sort of clothes-closet which housed a quantity of aprons and gowns, of buckets and pails and sundries. He was working his slow way round until his jailor had his back to it – it was like putting a billiard ball over a pocket. This done, he attacked the "Malabar" with almost inconceivable force, giving a pious grunt which echoed throughout the kitchen. Under the impetus of this rush the "Malabar", attentive to the threat of the knife, backed away and before he knew where he was found himself pinned into the closet against the hanging clothes, against the wall, with a hand firmly clutching his throat, his own arms vaguely encircling the shorter man with force but without design. And now Mnemidis with thoughtful and considered strokes, like an experienced cook, started to lard him with the knife he held in his hand. All this seemed to the "Malabar" to pass in a kind of languorous slow motion, but in fact the blows were swift and tellingly aimed. Meanwhile Mnemidis gazed into his face with attention, almost lecherously, as if he were looking into a gauge which might tell him how successful his assault was. Negroes do not turn pale but rosy in this kind of fatal situation. Mnemidis felt his man give a crooning sound and lean forward upon him. It would be like tearing down a high curtain, he thought to himself. Both were breathing heavily now, but Pierre was blowing out his cheeks with exhaustion, and his lungs were filling and emptying very quickly all of a sudden. It was as if he had run the 100 metres in record time.

With loving penetration Mnemidis continued to hold him and gaze up into his face, now bloodless and somehow serene despite the exhaustion – a serenity which perhaps counterfeited and anticipated the inevitable death which must follow such an exchange. It was a crucial sweetness, and the pallor was highly satisfying to the author of the assault who stood, holding him upright and scrutinising him so tenderly. At last Mnemidis stepped back and gently posed the teetering giant more snugly in the mass of hanging coats. He must be losing blood rapidly, Pierre, but he remained upright in a pose at once fragile and authoritative, his arms out and his fingers crooked, but no longer on the body of his adversary. His expression suggested that he was all of a sudden deeply introspective, investigating his inmost feelings; to try and determine perhaps the extent of the leak, the volume of blood which was now flowing – he could feel it, soft and quite insidious – flowing down. Losing blood, yes, he was losing *blood*. He groaned, and as if upon a signal Mnemidis stepped back and shut the closet door, leaving him to stand trembling among the clothes.

By the grace of the Creator the kitchens were still empty, he had them to himself; he was very thirsty, so he gave himself a long drink from the sink and tenderly wiped the blade of his knife. Then, squaring his shoulders, he went in search of a garment which might hide his nakedness above the waist, or indeed disguise him, for as yet his journey had only begun, there was much to be done. Vaguely stirring in the back of his mind was the idea of perhaps a chef's cape or a baker's white coat, or a doctor's regalia, but what he indeed hit upon was even more impenetrable as a disguise. Some of the nuns engaged in heavy manual labour like washing clothes or swabbing floors, had the habit of hanging up their robes and coifs in one of the adjacent changing-rooms which was open. He could hardly hide his glowing self-satisfaction as he found three or four of these costumes from which to choose; and most particularly the starched and all but spotless coifs. What a disguise! This huge headpiece was shaped like a lily and he slipped one on just to see how such an affair would look. He was amazed by his own face, it looked quite terrifyingly composed with just a trace of human light in the eye, and just a trace of a smile at the corners of the mouth. But he had never noticed before that he had dimples, and the better to study them he allowed his smile to broaden, to overflow as it were; the dimples belonged to someone's early childhood, as did the face now, whose contours were demarcated by the white helm of the nun. But this one was a trifle too big; he went along the line and out of the three or four available picked one which he snugged down over his head to make a perfect fit. Then he sought out the curtain-like nun's robes and picked a suitable one. All this happened in a flash; he consciously hurried things along because he could hear, somewhere in the depths of the building, a muffled bumping as if Pierre, half-foundered by the stabbing, had started to react, to fall about among the hanging coats.

The mirror gave back an elderly nun with a face full of unhealthy confessional secrets, expressions both perverted and hypocritical, but with an uncanny brilliance of eye. A nun of great experience, yet not disabused. A nun ready for anything. He almost chuckled with delight as he crept out of the closet and into the main hall, walking with bent head, as if deep in thought, and very slowly so as not to excite curiosity. He examined the notice-boards, passed them in review, and then just as self-confidently directed himself towards the wood which he traversed every day with Pierre. At once when he was under cover his pace increased, and he arrived at the little villa which housed the psychological unit almost at a run. By great good luck the office of Schwarz was empty, as also was the consulting-room of the woman doctor – the one he was most anxious to see. He sat down suddenly to reflect. Perhaps if he waited they might come, the one or the other? But the woman was more important.

He sat down in Schwarz's swivel chair for a long moment and reflected; in his mind he went back along the chain of past events – those of the last hour – in order to evolve a line of action suitable to his case and his intentions. He had retained the addresses of his two Egyptian friends, and once he had finished his scheduled business he intended to call at their hotel and give himself up, put himself in their charge, hoping that it was not too late for them to put the escape plan into operation and waft him back home to Cairo. So he sat, taking stock of himself and fingering the heavy handles of the kitchen knives – for he could not resist taking both. It was somewhat awkward having them, but each had a stout leather sheath and a scabbard, and each was attached by a tough thong so that he could loop it into the belt which held up his trousers. The long cassock-type garment of the nun was most voluminous, and obliterated all contours; it amused and excited him for it brought him back old memories of the carnivals in Alexandria. It was like a black domino. But . . . he sprang to his feet and chided himself for wasting valuable time here instead of moving on into town to further his plans. The nun's habit had two great inner pockets, one of which contained a rosary and the other tickets to a *fête votive* in a lake village. Not to mention a cambric handkerchief, with which he might cover part of his face if necessary. But it was a pity to have missed both the doctors like this. He felt a twinge of regret to leave the consulting-room without having, so to speak, made his mark, left a message of some sort. Yet what? On Schwarz's desk he saw an apple on a plate – it constituted the modest lunch of the analyst who was dieting and trying to lose weight. With his knife Mnemidis cut it in half, giving a little chuckle of pure mischief.

Then he set off at a trot through the wood, only slowing his pace when he came to open spaces bordering the main entrance, or trim gardens rich in flowerbeds where he adopted a loitering, contemplative gait, snail-like in fact, most suitable for a nun who tells her beads as she walks, rapt in prayerful union with her Saviour. He had expected by now some sort of spirited pursuit, cries of surprise, running footsteps; it was disappointing, but nevertheless. He was usually chased and pounced upon in such circumstances. But he recognised in all this the hand of fate – for he had as yet not accomplished his mission. He frowned as he walked thoughtfully towards the car park and the main entrance. There was a risk that the alarm had been given, that they had telephoned the front gate to stop all people trying to leave. But apparently not, all was quiet. It would be more than an hour before Pierre fell out of his cupboard on to the floor – under which the pool of blood had traced a path which someone would notice. No, all was normal in the office of the gate warden. Moreover, a further stroke of luck awaited the newly canonised nun, for parked outside the gate and obviously ready to move off was the baker's van which brought the establishment its daily bread. The driver, a fresh-faced youth, was just shutting down the motor hood after checking the oil. The sight of one of the sisters walking through the gate was not calculated to arouse any particular interest in the guardians of the gate who simply gave Mnemedis a cursory glance as he passed under their window. He held his handkerchief to his mouth as if he had a cold and spoke in a hoarse whisper as he asked the young driver whether he was going into town, and whether he would give him a lift to the lakeside village to the *fête votive* for which he had now two tickets. The boy agreed most respectfully to take the sister aboard, and Mnemidis climbed in beside him and snuggled down, delighted by the ease with which he had hoodwinked the authorities and broken prison. It was in the best tradition – he had never done a cleverer, smoother break-out in his whole life. He restrained a temptation to whistle a tune, and asked the young man in a hoarse whisper whether he went to church, and if so to which. "Catholic" was the reply.

Mnemidis was emboldened by the manifest impenetrability of his disguise – he looked every inch an elderly sister with a slightly waggish disposition. He took the wise precaution, however, of talking in a hoarse whisper, as if he had lost his voice, due to a heavy cold. As the nervous youth went on in *naïf* fashion to outline his religious convictions the sister of mercy put her arm about his shoulders in sacerdotal sympathy. Then she asked if during the night he was not troubled sometimes by unworthy thoughts or dreams or . . . wishes? And her hand slid softly down to caress the young man's thigh. He could not forbear to flush up and draw in his breath – it was sexually exciting to feel this apparently innocent advance. He did not quite know what to make of it. Meanwhile Mnemidis went on talking in his hoarse whisper about the difficulty of sleeping when one was young and pursued by chimeras of experiences one had not as yet tasted. Did not the young man sometimes . . . But the young man was manifestly excited now and blushing furiously. He had never had an experience of this order, and he had lost all his composure. After all, what could one say to a nun? He too felt that he had lost his voice, while the stealthy advance of the nun's hand now made clear her intention – of making free with him sexually. But the steady flow of language did not cease as the caresses became more pointed and deliberate. Finally, in a more authoritative fashion, the sister told him to pull his vehicle off the road and into a copse which obligingly presented itself, and here the seduction was consummated. The young man mixed confusion, sexual excitement and shame in equal parts. Then he conducted his passenger to the lakeside road and set her down at the gates of the park in which the *fête votive* was being held, and for which she held tickets, it would seem. The nun said goodbye with a ghoulish demureness and the young man drove off in something of a hurry, glad to be shot of so strange a customer.

But this encounter was most valuable to Mnemidis in that it gave him confidence in his disguise. It provoked no curiosity and much respect. He even tested it by going up to the policeman on the park gate and asking the time. The man drew back and saluted respectfully as he conveyed the information. No, it was completely foolproof. With a sigh of relief Mnemidis now abandoned himself to pure pleasure. He walked about the spacious gardens, visited the flower show in the conservatories and helped judge the competition by putting his judgement on to a slip of paper and sliding it into the box at the gate. Then he walked into the other corner and saw a Punch and Judy show which he found completely absorbing. He had forgotten how marvellous the facial expressions of children can be when they are absorbed by a theatrical performance. You can see the adult lodged in the youthful body; if you gaze into the eyes and let your intelligence flow into the child's face you can divine very clearly what sort of adult it will become in due course. He was delighted by this exercise, involving a thesaurus of young faces in all their moods. And then he went into a concert where gross romantic music was the keynote, and he throbbed and almost swooned to the strains of Strauss and Delibes. Emotion is permitted in a nun. He moved his head from side to side and closed his eyes with each wave of delight. At the same time his fingers caressed the forms of the knives which lay so quietly obedient upon his thighs.

He had all the time in the world, that is what he had begun to feel. He could afford to take his time. But when he spotted a telephone booth he suddenly remembered that he did not yet know the exact address of Constance's flat. But he soon found her in the supplement devoted to trades and professions, and reading over the address a couple of times unerringly memorised it.

This is where he would go when he was good and ready, to exact retribution from the woman who had so misused him both morally and physically. He closed his eyes the better to memorise the address.

FIVE

The Return Journey

WITHIN THE SPACE OF THIS RELATIVELY SHORT absence from the town Constance found that the dispositions had somewhat changed, been reshuffled. The mid-morning "elevenses" of Toby and Sutcliffe had remained the only constant, but the company of the *billiard-aires*, as Sutcliffe had christened what threatened now to become an informal club, had been increased by new arrivals. Blanford had graduated to a wheel-chair with a movable back which he could adjust to correspond to his waves of fatigue, or desire for a cat-nap. He found the atmosphere most congenial for his work, and he found that Sutcliffe argued best when he was allowed to be slightly absent-minded, half-concentrated on a tricky shot. He had his best thoughts paradoxically when he was occupied with something else – it was as if they were completely involuntary, arriving from nowhere: but every artist has this unique experience, of receiving throbs from outer space as pure gifts. Another member of the company was Max, who in a curious way felt a little lonely in Geneva and was anxious to take up old friendships; he played an excellent game of pool, and despite his new avocation as a yogi was still very much his old self, easy to tease in an affectionate way for he was so very humble, had always been despite the gaudy uniforms provided by Lord Galen. The gloomy and deteriorate old bar took on a new life; the moribund old man who ran it so very inexpertly invoked the aid of a niece or a daughter-in-law who started to produce eatable comestibles and superior brands of whisky and gin to meet the new custom. And this general disposition towards improvement had borne fruit, for among the new members of this confraternity were two of the secretaries who worked for Toby, and even Ryder, Sutcliffe's head of section, who since his wife's accident had taken to drinking rather heavily. Moreover, he was somewhat intimidated, or so he professed, by frequenting "sort of artist chaps", because he was simply "an ordinary lowbrow service mind". His misgivings were rudely set to rest by Sutcliffe.

"The word is a misnomer, it should be *autist.* I know that the animal is short of manners and lacks true refinement, but then he is tolerably happy with his vulgar streak. There are advantages in being a *parvenu*: one is shunned by people dying of the slow blood-poisoning of over-refinement. The poor artist is a fartist, and he belongs to an endangered species and needs the protection of the reservation. His compensations are secret ones. He belongs to the Floppy Few!"

"O Christ!" said the soldier in despair. "If ever there was someone in need of subtitles . . ."

But it was not always as bad as this, and he solaced himself with the more worldly company of Felix Chatto who had smelt out this informal morning gathering and graced it with his company several times a week. Geneva was short on really good company combined with complete informality, and that is what the smoky little bar had to offer, despite its impersonality and general ugliness. And the general relaxation of the atmosphere was also a sign that the long suppurating war was drawing to an end. New sorts of agency were beginning to make their appearance in the town – agencies for peace and reconstruction, not for war, espionage, subversion. The faintest shadow of a new atmosphere had begun to flower among the ruins of the epoch. Yet how exhausted they all were. (These thoughts are those of Constance.) Yes, even those who had apparently done nothing were worn down by the invisible moral attrition of war. In her own case she felt its separate weight added to the weight of the human experiences through which she had found her way with such difficulty, with so many hesitations. And now once more changes were in the air, the structure of things was shifting, disintegrating around her. Soon, she supposed dumbly, she would be on the move again, heading for some distant country, some new project. Only the thought that Affad was coming back halted her.

"Halted her" is not true either, for at the very heart of her emotion, the seat of her loving awareness of him as a man, she was aware that something had gone wrong and that she did not know how it could be put right; it was like a break in an electrical circuit, it would need mending by both sides. But if they were not together? There was the rub. To still her sense of overwhelming boredom she had begun to spend more time with Blanford, indeed whole afternoons talking to him on his balcony or lying beside his bed. Not infrequently they were joined by the massive figure of Sutcliffe, tired of pacing the waterfront on misty afternoons. It was curious, too, to hear them discussing the interminable sequences of the "double concerto" as Blanford called their novel now. He took the concerns of form very seriously and reacted with annoyance to Sutcliffe's jocose suggestions, namely that the whole thing would be much tidier as an exchange of letters. "We could have fun, spelling God backwards! You could sign yourself OREPSORP and I could sign myself NABILAC. It's the other side of the moon for Prospero and Caliban – between us we could really control things. I mean Reality or YTILAER. With many an involuntary chuckle and lots of spicy new dialogue like: 'A stab of grog, Podsnap – I mean Pansdop? Don't mind if I do, mate. Couldn't care less if I did!' In this way *enanteiodromion*, everything would be seen to be turning into its opposite, even our book which would take on a mighty shifty strangeness, become an enticement for sterile linguists to parse in their sleep."

"But hard on the reader, surely," pleaded Constance. "And of an unhealthy schizoid cast of mind."

Aubrey said, "I am deliberately turning the novel inside out like a sleeve."

"Then back," said Sutcliffe.

"Yes, then back."

"I have treated people like you, sometimes even much worse. But with no success, alas. And I was brought up on rigorous fare like Ivanhoe and Proust which enjoyed classical exactitude as to form . . ."

"But that is Culture," said Sutcliffe in his most reproachful manner. "Or if you prefer, ERUTLUC. You see, we have never been interested in the real world – we see it through a cloud of disbelief. Ni eht gninnigeb saw eht drow!" He intoned the phrase majestically and explained that it was simply the backspelling of "In the beginning was the Word!"

"So we are back to culture, are we?" she said. "And we are not the only ones. Lord Galen is being deeply troubled by the word as well."

Blanford said, "I know. He has been to see me about it. But first let me tell you about Cade my manservant who has started to encounter him at night when he prowls about the city. Cade, when he is deeply thinking, puts on an extraordinary facial expression which reminds me of that sculpture by an artist whose name I have repressed called 'Romulus and Remus founding Rome'. That is how intense it is. Then after a time he clears his throat and says, 'Sir, may I speak?' and when I nod, goes on, 'I saw *him* again last night!' A hush. 'Him who?' I ask and he says with slyness, 'Lord Galen. He was in one of the houses. They were laughing at him. They asked me if he was really a Lord because he calls his balls his "heirlooms". Of course, I said, that's why he is worried about their performance. He 'opes for a son and heir. I trust I was right, I done right.' 'Cade, you done right.' 'Thank you, Master Aubrey.' "

"I shall ask Toby to take Galen to the Swiss perverts' restaurant where they only serve fried grapes in order to break down your reserve. Is he really worried about his heirlooms?"

"No. It's to do with culture. And it is very human and touching. He has been told to see man in the raw!"

Indeed there was a good deal of truth in this, and it had largely come about because of Galen's latest and most illustrious appointment.

He sidled into Blanford's room at the clinic looking like the Phantom of the Opera; there were dark circles under his eyes. He was slightly out of breath and very much out of composure as he cast about for a way of expressing his disturbed feelings. "Aubrey!" he said, with a suspicion of a quiver to his underlip, "I felt that I must consult you, and I hope you will have time to hear me out. Aubrey, I am at a great crossroads in my professional life." He sat down on a chair, and placing a briefcase full of books on the floor at his feet, fanned himself with his hat – as if to quell the fires of anxiety which were consuming him. "My dear Lord Galen, of course," said Blanford with a rush of affection and sympathy, and put out his hand which Galen grabbed and shook with gratitude. "What is it? What can it be?"

Galen allowed his breathing to rediscover its normal rhythm before unfolding his tale. "Today, Aubrey," he said at last, "I am at the top of the tree, I have the plum job of all – I am the Coordinator of Coordinated Cultures!" He waited for it to sink in before continuing, "And yet I can't for the life of me discover what culture *is*, what the word I am in charge of *means*. I know that I pass for a well-educated man and all that. But I am supposed to work out a report which will deal with the whole future of the European book, for example, for we control all the paper. Someone has to decide what is good of our culture, and that is me. But how can I decide if I don't know what it is? And from every side they come bringing me what they call 'cornerstones' to look at. 'You must include that in your recommendations, it's a *cornerstone*,' they keep saying.

I am surrounded with cornerstones. And some of them – well, I have never been so disgusted in my life." He groped among his affairs and produced a copy of *Ulysses* by Joyce. "Aubrey! Upon my honour what do you think of this . . . this cornerstone?"

"I can see your dilemma," said Aubrey, thinking of the scabrous parts of Joyce's masterpiece. But to his surprise what Galen said was, "It's the most anti-Semitic book I have ever read. Absolutely *virulent*." Aubrey was quite bemused for he had never read it in this way. "Just how?" he asked in genuine perplexity and Lord Galen hissed back, "If as they tell me the earliest cornerstone was Homer with his hero Ulysses, representing the all-wise and all conquering traveller, the European human spirit so to speak, why this book is a wicked take-off of Homer, a satire. According to Joyce the modern Ulysses is a Dublin Jew of the most despicable qualities, the lowest character, the foulest morals; and his wife even lower. This is what our civilisation has come to . . ." He made the noise which is represented in French novels phonetically as "*Pouagh!*"

He poured himself a very stiff whisky and made a forlorn gesture of impotence, as if invoking either the sky or perhaps the shade of Joyce himself to descend and resolve his dilemma. But Blanford was genuinely aroused by this extraordinary analysis, the first of its kind, and lost in admiration mixed with astonishment that such insight came from someone like Galen. In a flash his mind seized on the notion and fitted it into a scheme which might satisfy a philosopher of culture of the kind of Spengler. European Man as the gay artificer Ulysses who had endured until Panurge took up the tale once more and made it live. And then the Dionysiac force gradually spent itself and the Spenglerian decline and division set in. Expiring volcanoes went on smoking with names like Nietzsche, Strindberg, Tolstoy, but the ship was going down by the stern . . . Lord Galen was there, floating in the sky with his arms outspread, a look of agonised perplexity on his face, crying, "Our culture! What is it? I wish someone could tell me." In his hand another "cornerstone", another virulently anti-Semitic analysis of European culture with its bias towards materialism and the inevitable exploitation of the underprivileged by the "capitalists". Céline! The form of Lord Galen settled once more like a moth upon the end of the bed to continue his exposition. "Now at last this beastly war caused by that rotter Hitler is actually coming to an end and we can hope for peace, we can work for peace. Aubrey, my dear boy, can't you see what hope there is in the air? A real hope! But if our culture goes on being celebrated by fanatical anti-Semites we shall end in another bloodbath – O God. My goodness, what have the Jews done to merit it? After all we gave you our bomb to drop on the Japanese. Our very own bomb which we could have kept to ourselves, or else charged you an enormous royalty on its use while keeping the patent private. Don't you see? But this problem came at me head on when I got my new post. For about ten years, as far as we can see, there will have to be some sort of priority system of control for paper stocks. Not only sanitary paper, Aubrey, but also school textbooks as well as newspapers and books of art. Above all 'cornerstones'. The question to ask oneself is always 'Is it a cornerstone or not? If not, out!' The whole thing has become a nightmare and has caused the whole of my committee days of acrimonious argument, and myself anxiety and sleeplessness. But I owe it to European culture to get it right. I must pass the books which are fruitful and proscribe those which aren't. But how to decide? It's all very well to suggest, as someone did, that we might get a book like this *Ulysses* rewritten in a more acceptable and forward-looking manner by someone like Beverley Nicholls, but that would be interfering, and I don't hold with mere temporising measures. You cannot rewrite a cornerstone or even bowdlerise it; I quite agree and would never condone it. But how to be sure what is what? I received a petition from the committee which said: 'In our view our Chairman for all his experience of commerce and diplomacy has a somewhat narrow view of culture and ordinary life. In our view he should perhaps go out into the world a little and see man as he is, in the raw, in order to judge the culture of which he is only a part.' I try not to get too easily nettled and I accepted the criticism in good part. Well, I must go out more into the world. But first I rang up Schwarz and asked him if he knew why everyone was so anti-Semite, and he said, yes, he did. It was because of monotheism and monolithic radical philosophies based on the theory of values. It was Judaism, he said, that irritated everyone so. He added that I was behaving like a paranoid minority syndrome in allowing myself to get upset. Aubrey, I have been called many things in my time but never a syndrome. I rang off in despair. This is what you get when you search quite disinterestedly for the meaning of a word like culture in our time."

He halted the recital of his woes in order once more to avail himself of the whisky which, Blanford remarked, he now drank in heroic doses, hardly diluted. It was obvious that this intellectual adventure had shaken him, had even pushed him into having recourse to the bottle more frequently than was his wont. "And then what?" said Aubrey, torn between amusement and sympathy for his friend. Galen groaned. "Schwarz," he said, "has got an amazing idea that the Jews *created* racial discrimination by their Chosen Race policy and their refusal to dilute the superior blood of Israel by mixing it with inferior brands. Isn't that very strange?" Aubrey said, "Well, it's one way of looking at it. It could be true like in India; the top dog complex creates instant Untouchables – which is what the gentiles are for strict Jews. Am I wrong?" Galen knew nothing of India. "Jews are not all Untouchables, on the contrary they are very generous, though of course they bargain and like to know where their money goes. But the Jew is generous, quite an easy touch in fact!"

There seemed no point in pursuing this line of thought, based as it was on a typical misunderstanding. "You win," said Aubrey, abandoning the train of thought, and with a smile Lord Galen stretched out along the end of the bed and, metaphorically, put his head under his wing and went to sleep, looking rather like an old rook snoozing on its nest.

But he went on talking with his eyes shut – burbling, rather, for there were patches of free association as well as gaps in the slow sequence of his rambling. It was as if he were talking not to Aubrey but to his Maker. For example, at one point he raised his head and still with closed eyes exclaimed passionately, "No Gentile could have invented double-entry bookkeeping!" accompanying the thought with a gesture of fearful vehemence. Now, however, he subsided into sleep with a somewhat fatuous smile on his face and whispered, "It was all this that led me to the *pouf* of Mrs Gilchrist. A young diplomat in search of profound sensations agreed to accompany me. I did not know of her international celebrity at the time – apparently like so many things in our time she is a chain store, and has branches all over India, Turkey, Greece, France and Eastbourne. She literally breeds girls for the diplomatic and military markets. I seemed to impress her very favourably; she said I had majesty. She was of uncertain age and with heavily tinted hair combined joviality and hysterectomy in equal parts. For a moment I almost thought I might love such a woman – Aubrey, they were right, I was in need of wantonness. She was, said my young diplomat friend, thoroughly representative of the age and the culture, so I could go ahead and explore on an empirical basis. There was a lot of talk about Lective (hic) Finities – another cornerstone by Goitre. I didn't follow but pretended I did until she hopped back on the nest. Then I was lost in the night of her hair – afternoon, rather, it was bright red. But lost, lost to reason. I had heard of whirlwind romances before but never realised fully. I tell you this, Aubrey, because I don't want to hide anything from you, I want your views on culture. And besides, you know all, for in the midst of this adventure who should I meet but your man Cade who said to me, 'Lor' bless you, Milord, what are you doing in a place like this? With Mrs Gilchrist! It's like fucking a dead mouse.' He is a coarse and narrow-minded man and doesn't know what it is to empty some dull opiate, as my young diplomatic friend puts it. But things went from bad to worse for when we returned to what Mrs Gilchrist called the winter garden there were a lot of half-dressed people dancing in a marked way, some with few if any clothes. One young man in an apron and a boater, who had a flower behind each ear, stubbed out a cigar on my forearm without asking permission. The pain was terrible. I still have the scar. Another dressed in next to nothing forced me to waltz and gave me a bite on the cheek which kept me from the office for a week. Mrs Gilchrist said it was nothing, just a love-at-first-sight-bite. I was by now in an advanced condition of intemperance and not much able to look after myself. But I was making mental notes all the time. She had covered my neck in what in such circles are known as *suçons d'amour*, blue marks. But she seemed proud of me for I heard her proclaim, 'Celui-là a des couilles superposées.' I wondered what my committee would say if they could see me. Well, whose fault was it? There was a kind of fight, and an influx of policemen and it was then I saw your man, who kindly helped me to the door. I found myself in the street sitting on the pavement with my opera hat beside me – someone had jumped on it – and being bandaged by some of the nicer girls: but of course they were going through my pockets and wallet. However, I had taken the precaution of carrying very little money and no personal jewellery of value; my signet I left in the office safe. So that all in all, while I was shorn, it was not completely. My diplomatic friend put me in a cab and – against my will – took me to another dingier place where I got stuck in the lavatory and was kicked by a curate. I protested, whereupon my friend said, 'Are you a man of the world or no?' 'Yes!' 'Well then!' I didn't see his point."

There was a long pause, some snoring and the dazed voice once more took up the tenuous thread of what now seemed to be a jag lasting over weeks; perhaps it was just the confusion in the telling. "O my God! how she talked and talked about culture. And I kept telling myself that I must remember everything in order to report to the committee. O my God!" He groaned again and wagged his head on his shoulders.

"Thelème!" he said once more. "I don't suppose the name means anything to you. An abbey somewhere in Provence, the abode of perfected felicity! It is now called Cuculotte in the Gard, centre of the hot chestnuts trade. Mrs Gilchrist sometimes goes down at Easter with her mother. Her belly is cloven with the devil's hoofmark, but her sex is as smooth or smoother than a surgeon's glove. Sometimes she turns down the lights and does horoscopes. She can see auras, she can overhear states of mind. When I told Sutcliffe this he said, 'Let everyone make his personal noise for the braying of donkeys is sweet to the ears of the Creator!' Cuculotte, she saw it so clearly in a dream. There is a woman waiting for me there who looks like the Virgin Mary but is really called Cunégonde – another cornerstone. A hole-and-cornerstone. Ha! Ha! My diplomatic youth again, the poor cynic. I last saw him standing naked, on Mrs Gilchrist's upper balcony, arms wide as he declaimed, 'Hear me, ye sperm-coaxing divinities, for I am afflicted by scrotum fever and I bring ye my purse of Fortunatus!' The Swiss fire brigade had to get him down with a ladder and I expect he has been rusticated already. O God, Aubrey, all this because they said I had not lived enough.

"But *Ulysses*, that odious book, what is one to do? Toby

says that all energetic wanderers descend from Dionysus, they are really gods of wine which gives warmth and motion and curiosity. The wandering Jew, the Flying Dutchman, Gil Blas, Panurge – O my head spins with everything I have been hearing!"

Aubrey thought with a pang of the long nightmare of Joyce's struggle to get his work published – eighteen years – and said, "You must not blacklist him, whatever you find to say against it, you must not index Joyce. The Catholics already did, and he was a secret Catholic as much marked as old Huysmans ever was. Hence the heavy liturgical type of prose exposition with its gruesome echoes and parodies of what he could not forget. No, it's rich in church furnishings, and the function of Bloom is to desecrate the Church, to shit on the High Altar. You are lucky if he doesn't recite the Creed as he shits. No, it's a real cornerstone."

But this time Galen slept and did not hear; faint snores escaped his lips though he still smiled at some cherished memory; and it was during this period that the shadow of Sutcliffe tiptoed into the room, finger on lip, and took up an amused position in a nearby chair, whispering, "Is it okay for me to be here – or is he confessing all?"

"Nearly all. He speaks of a Mrs Gilchrist whom I seem to have heard of."

"Of course. Those songs. The first scowling clap brought back from Gallipoli by the Anzacs was claimed by one of her girls. The song was plaintive – Will she give you the cherry off the cake, Mrs Gilchrist?"

"I never heard it."

"I could bring her to have tea with you; she probably does massage as well."

"Thank you, my friend, but no."

"With me too she waxes mystical and speaks movingly of the Third Eye, Troisième Oeil as she says with a classy twitch. But what really concerns her is the Troisième Jambe of men – those who had it were marvellous. 'Quel homme fascinant, il est géomètre', she would coo. Or else, 'un homme spécial; il est chef de gare mais il a des qualités de coeur!' She is what our ancestors would call an adept of splosh-fucking. As Cade would say, 'She'd fuck the tiles off the roof if you let her.'"

"I did not know you had shared this tremendous binge of Galen's." Sutcliffe nodded and said, "The real life of Geneva, capital of Calvin, goes on there. Toby found it, and it proved so restful that he often takes his knitting down for an hour and just sits, listening to the banter of Mrs Gilchrist's girls. It is the hub of this Spenglerian capital where one sees that our civilisation is the weary little monkey which sits atop the barrel organ and proffers a tin cup for alms while the organ-grinder is a large Jewish gentleman of urbanity. Toby says that Freud is the only honest Jew, just as Socrates was the only honest Greek. Yes, I have been sharing in the quest for the Golden Fleece – if I may call it that. And a fine job he has made of it. He has discovered that when the love of lamb cutlets is universal the reign of benevolence will begin. A thermonuclear Jehovah is watching over us!"

"There's a hellish lack of continuity in what you say."

"It's good sense but somewhat diluted with whisky. It will all get clearer and clearer – now that you have admitted to yourself that I exist – or rather that you only exist in function to me! Socrates only existed in Plato's mind, Freud only in Jung's, that's how the whole thing goes. It's a chain gang. Sam once had a limerick about the matter which went:

> Who sends out his cock to the Cleaner's
> Must risk quite a shrinking of penis
> Which perhaps is restored
> By recourse to a bawd
> And a subsequent transit of Venus."

"Be more precise, please; you rave!"

"It is very simple, Aubrey: if the Superego is really God the Father, then man is the only animal who has one ball higher than the other – no other carries his ingots in this position. The women have found out and here they are jousting, tossing the caber, climbing the greasy pole, wrestling in mud, writing, painting, pissing standing up, clearing their throats just like – better than – men. I am fordolked, *morfondu*, chilled to the heart by the spectacle. This is what comes of letting them share the war."

"But at least they are free and you can get at them."

"In a manner of speaking." He recited darkly the verse:

> Marsupial Sutcliffe with distinguished balls
> Sits by the telephone and waits for calls.

For a moment, like a whale surfacing, the recumbent figure of Lord Galen condensed itself and shot upright as if on a spring. "My God, where am I?" he asked in total bewilderment, and then just as suddenly closed his eyes and sank back into profound sleep once more. Aubrey said, "If he can sleep through your disquisitions he can sleep through anything."

"I haven't told you all as yet," went on Sutcliffe in a hushed voice after having allowed Galen a moment or two to engulf himself thoroughly in slumber. "I haven't told you about the Crucifixion on the most memorable evening, the last and worst. At midnight or after there came an influx of theatre people, or perhaps a carnival party, with extravagant hats and plumes and weird noses and masks. They were all more or less drunk and the naked sirens of the house had great fun in plucking their clothes from them like fruit from trees, appropriating their hats and noses and whatnot, while the whole place resounded with music and everyone fell to the knife and fork act with celerity, except for those like little Cravache-Biche who must be corrected with nettles. Don't tell me where they found them at this time of night, perhaps by moonlight near the lake. In all this the wistful Galen wandered vaguely half-undressed and on the incoherent side of his last huge whisky. There was a sudden fight, too, which was not allowed to deteriorate into fisticuffs, thank goodness, though I heard a female voice cry raucously, 'Lâche-moi, espèce de morve,' which I translated back to myself as meaning: 'Unhand me, species of snot!' The contestants were separated by two clowns and the party rolled on over our heads like the sea. More players, more music – a kind of predynastic jazz with sweet unction of clarinets calling from forgotten minarets to the faithful who crowded the tiny dance floor yapping like Pekinese. Someone was crying 'Redemption!' and I thought he was a religious maniac, but no, he was waving a banker's draft: yes, there were bankers among us, and I even saw one undressed. He looked just like other men but he was crying, 'I am absolutely frozen, my ingots, my heirlooms, my assets are frozen, I tell you.' It was not clear whom he was trying to convince. Toby was talking moodily of bringing down a secret transmitter to the *pouf* in order to sift all the available information. 'Why not install it – I sometimes have brilliant ideas – in Mrs Gilchrist's pussy? From there you command the whole wide world.'

"But I had no chance to develop my idea for a fascinating dark girl intervened and coaxed me into indulging in some conventional knife and fork in an alcove – the facsimile of a joy I would gladly have shared with her. She was of a dark, grave, Semitic beauty, and in distress, thrilling like a wounded nerve. And I felt my age heavy upon me as I gazed into those sweet wounded eyes. Aïe! Jewish girls have fur-lined pussies and simmer with sinful single-mindedness, salacious and solitary and sexual as swallows in spring: they swerve out of the dark syllabaries of sensuality with superb submission like silken scimitars swung by a sultan . . ."

"Wow!"

"Thank you so much!"

"Tell me about love. I have been forbidden it since I have been here and I am beginning to miss it. This nun's life is bad for my book. I fear that if too long out of use one surely atrophies, no?"

"I don't think so – ask your doctor."

"I have and he says not. Actually I am less worried for myself than for my baby, my book. Ah, Rob, what a strange obsession it is, this writing game! I desire the sovereign form exposed by exact method – open-cast mining, or better, heart surgery. But in order to achieve it you must first get mental pruritus, the desire to *know*, and then quietly scratch yourself to death, the paper to death with your pen. And all to what end?"

"Well, if you can't love it's your only alibi."

The thought was displeasing to Blanford, so in order to cheer him up Sutcliffe recited:

> Another lovely morning in the history of Our Saviour,
> I pray you children one and all, be on your best behaviour.
> Put all these problems out to grass
> And watch the generations pass.
> I've lived my life, I've had my say,
> A lucky dog, I've had my day.
> Rise early, darlings, catch the dew
> And may you join the Happy Few.

"What is really ailing you is a theological nagging which has little to do with your book, since it is neither a *plaidoyer* nor does it preach anything. But if you go mucking about with the discrete ego you must be careful not to make a mistake and release a whole lot of indiscreet ids. Remember that a conjuror must be worthy of his balls!"

"Well said! Nobly said!"

"And now, Aubrey, to my main theme. It is nothing less

than the Crucifixion of Lord Galen at the hands of Mrs Gilchrist and her girls, a sight of great dramatic and symbolic significance. It is amazing with what modesty and good nature he went to his doom; indeed, he chose his own doom, but it was very late in the night, towards the third hour when different realities begin to sift into each other and the Chinese distinguish finely between the day particle and the night particle, between the definite and indefinite article. There came a young lady to the door of the apartment clad in nothing but a sort of drunken dignity who raised her voice and said, 'There is a Jewish gentleman below who wishes to be crucified and has asked me if you will all oblige.' There was an immediate rush of willingness to please, everyone felt warm and generously disposed, but how to proceed? There were no nails to be found anywhere, lucky for Galen. Meanwhile, where was he actually? For some time past he had not been in evidence and one presumed him to have left or fallen asleep in some nook. But instead he had been undressed and locked into a cupboard full of brooms and slop-pails and here, after announcing his determination to expiate the sins of Jewry by getting himself crucified, he waited with smiling patience. The girl in question having prepared her audience now released him and led him unprotestingly from room to room – he smiling bashfully and somewhat roguishly the while: but he was drunk beyond deadness, beyond coma, beyond the seventh sphere of incomprehension. He was hazed in, worn out and living in a world of his own. He was nude and his Old Etonian tie had been attached to his principal member, and it was with this that he was led, just as Gandhi led his goat through the market-place where he received a resounding ovation. It was as if a Turkish butcher might lead a succulent fat-tailed sheep across the market place in order to beat up his clients' saliva by the spectacle. Our own saliva flowed copiously enough, but where was the impedimenta – the cross, for example? We did not know that it was not the first time that Mrs Gilchrist had organised a little crucifixion to please an exacting client – but that we supposed would be perverse, perhaps, catering to special inclinations. Galen looked too naively happy to be a pervert, lusting after red-hot pincers or beds of nails. He turned his head from side to side as he walked through the rooms in harmless beatitude and one could not help being charmed and wishing him well in his little adventure.

"The girl having trailed her cape, so to speak, throughout the various salons, made her way, followed by a considerable crowd of enthusiasts, to the high walled-in verandah which Mrs Gilchrist called the Quarterdeck. The only furniture was a huge double bed with massive medieval baldaquin, which stood in the middle of what seemed a sort of nuptial chamber. Perhaps it was here in this mammoth bed that a youthful Mrs Gilchrist had yielded to the charms of the now phantom Major, whom she was wont to invoke as her late husband? At all events this was to be the site of Galen's crucifixion, for the two thick bedposts served admirably as struts upon which they could string him – better, indeed, than a cross, though a trifle less symmetrical as to the feet. However the concourse of maidens with cries and songs and expressions of goodwill now started to lash his outspread arms to the posts while in a Christ-like enfeeblement but with good humour Galen's head lolled and he expatiated upon himself: 'I wanted only to be good, pious and obedient,' he confessed modestly, 'I was prepared to wait for God to make me original. My dears, it worked. It worked and here I am!' He tried to spread his arms in triumph but was impeded by his fastenings. But he was not discountenanced, for he continued: 'The Ambassador to Bangalore appeared before me dressed in the robes of a *khitmagar* or majordomo. He said: "Why don't you refuse the whole blood-stained Christian package, eh? Doff the butcher's apron so to speak, refuse the self-righteous futility of it all, stop being a martyr to respectability, dissociate yourself from blood-gulpers and wafer-chewers with their smithereens complex. Zonk! Bonkers! Pliouc! Be yourself even in strip cartoons! My dear Galen, relinquish your ghastly monotheism which has led to man's separation from nature and released the primal devastator in him. Pierce to the heart of helplessness, of harmlessness, which is Buddhism. Let meditation be the mould of feeling and breath the engine of thought!"'

"In the midst of all the horseplay and noise Galen did succeed in looking something like a Mantegna Christ Crucified – all except for the foolish good humour with which he submitted to an occasional tickle in the ribs. Or else a passing girl might seize his Old Etonian tie and give a tug, crying out 'Ding-Ding!' in the accents of a passing tram. Or yet another might cry out, 'They say he has dimples in his bottom like a French novelist!' But in the intervals the noble lord went on reciting the interminable Buddhist creed – for that is what it sounded like to the onlookers. 'Guilelessly, harmlessly, heedlessly, noiselessly, needlessly, haplessly, hopelessly, toplessly, shapelessly, soundlessly, stainlessly . . .'

"At this very moment who should come upon the scene but Mrs Gilchrist herself, wrapped in a whorl of pink silk and white fur, and winnowing her way across the floor like a wild bird dragging its claws across the surface of a lake: she skidded into view exuding majesty and a certain reproachfulness. Clapping her hands loudly she was exclaiming, 'My children! My children! What is going on? Why aren't things being hurried up? What about the *extermination* of the Jewish gentleman?' And with this she chucked Galen familiarly under the chin, causing him to giggle once more – though his expression was ever so slightly tinged with alarm – for he clearly did not know what the word might connote in the mind of Mrs Gilchrist. But for the girls it contained no secret. At once from behind their backs there appeared lipsticks of various types and hues – lipsticks like the little red sex of a thousand lapdogs lusting for love. And now the girls swarmed all over Lord Galen, decorating him with intense concentration, covering every available nook of his august person with flowers, mottoes, cobwebs, hearts, arrows, as well as other less familiar *graffiti*, like the genitalia of other members of the animal kingdom famed for their lubricity. It was a veritable fertility rite which was accomplished with almost no bickering, while the subject stayed rapturously still with arms outspread, feeling for the first time in his life thoroughly appreciated, thoroughly loved and understood. But from time to time fatigue overwhelmed him and he sagged briefly in his lashings. Then came catastrophe.

"In order to draw on his back and his bottom, not to mention his legs, the young ladies of Mrs Gilchrist climbed upon the bed in force, and it would seem that this was responsible for what followed. The heavy baldaquin, worked out of true by their wrigglings, suddenly broke away from the frame and crashed down, carrying one upright with it – fortunately Lord Galen was propelled sideways out of reach of the falling pieces and thus avoided an extremely nasty knock on the head. But he still remained tied by one arm, feebly draped across the floor. There was not an inch of his person that had escaped the artistic enthusiasm of the girls and he really looked like a tattooed Maori warrior prepared for a battle, or some obscure African chief prepared to preside at a witch cult. There was, of course, a delicious panic now, with bumps and bruises and squeaks all round, and when it was clear that for the moment the rest of the bed held firm, the girls who had drawn back now closed in once more upon Lord Galen and helped him down from the cross with strokings and mewings and consoling cries lest he had been frightened by the accident. He had, of course, but in a vague way, his whole sensibility deadened by drink. So now they carried the crucified and exterminated one to a nearby sofa and laid him out in vaguely ceremonial fashion, piling cushion upon cushion on him, and leaving only his grotesquely decorated head to stick out – it was like burying a Red Indian totem pole. But it was lovely and warm with the weight of the cushions upon him and he snuggled down in great good humour, confident that he would rise again on the third day because Mrs Gilchrist informed him that he would. 'Have a little kip, dear,' she suggested. But it was not to be.

"At that moment, with the air of avenging angels, two forms appeared as if by magic, stilling the tumult with a gesture of doom. One was the transfigured form of Felix Chatto, white with shock and resentment and outrage. In his hand he waved – an appropriate symbol of disapprobation – his London gamp meticulously rolled. He carried it high, just as Zeus might carry his trident or a saint his sceptre. And he shouted in a slightly daft voice which broke under the stress of his emotion, '*This has got to stop once and for all!*' The message was meant in particular for Galen but it was propelled with sufficient force to include the whole of the company. The second figure, who looked abashed and out of place, was, of all people, Schwarz who stood about disconsolately waving a stomach pump – he had been misled about Galen's condition which continued to register a mild euphoria despite the rather terrifying nature of his decorations. Felix was almost dancing with rage, his sense of *que dira-t-on* had been increasingly exacerbated as day followed day and rumour rumour about Galen's cultural researches. 'The whole of Geneva is laughing at you!' he cried and with his gamp struck at the recumbent figure, but hitting him through the cushions which gave out a satisfactory thwack. Galen's painted face worked – writhed, one might say – within its decorative scheme. He vaguely sensed that he was in a position of inferiority and just as vaguely thought to redress the situation with a reproof. 'I never expected to see you in a place like this, Felix,' he said in hollow tones, and the exacerbated young man hissed back, 'And you? I came here to find *you*, and I have brought a doctor and an ambulance. This time you will be disintoxicated once and for all in the best clinic of Geneva!' Lord Galen shrugged and threw up his hands; his underlip wobbled, and for a moment he looked as if he were on the edge of tears. 'You are judging me very harshly,' he said, with a shake of the head, 'After all I have been through, you are judging me *very* harshly.'

"Felix, still brandishing his umbrella, said, 'Someone had to do something. This last month has been a nightmare. At every turn I ran into one of your subcommittees asking for news of you, or worse still *giving* me news of your behaviour – highly unpalatable news, if I may so.'

"Felix, it is at their prompting that I undertook this path. If you knew what I have been through – dear boy, simply the American novel, nothing else! God! what a feast of violence and vulgarity and slime. I could hardly believe my eyes. And every one a cornerstone! No, Felix, there is a Communist Index and a Catholic Index and so far so good. Now I am going to establish Galen's graduated scale of acceptability and see if the United Nations will bite. God, but I am tired!' And now he had begun to look it. It was as if for the first time he realised fully that he was completely tattooed with lipstick. He gazed down at himself and gave the ghost of a whinny – the very last shadow of an exhausted chuckle. 'Well, if I must I must!' he said and held out his arms.

"For a moment there was some hesitation as to how he should be clothed for his departure from Mrs Gilchrist's establishment; but two interns appeared bearing a stretcher and having carefully wrapped him in sheets he was lowered into it, and covered with a blanket. The girls made a good deal of petting him and Mrs G. took her farewell with a light and airy kiss. And so Galen's search for culture ended."

A pause now ensued and all eyes were once more focused

on the sleeping man who had not turned a hair throughout the hushed disquisition of Sutcliffe. It was rather the silence which woke him now, and very quietly. He raised his head and said, "You were talking about me? Yes, I felt it."

He yawned luxuriously and went on: "For the first time I feel really rested, completely cured. It's been wonderfully therapeutic just lying on your feet and resting – I hope I didn't crush? No? Good!" Indeed he looked once more his old expansive, convivial self as he rose and put his clothes to rights and combed his hair. "This afternoon and evening," he said, "I must face the Central Committee with my recommendations, and we will know all!" He took up his bag full of cultural "cornerstones" and took his leave. A tight-lipped and unforgiving Felix awaited him in the car outside the clinic, ready to drive him to his office, and to make sure that he did not escape again.

"I fear," said Sutcliffe, "that this is the end of Galen the polymath and cultural dictator. I hear from Toby that he is collecting massive votes of no-confidence inside his own party, and that that monstrous ass Gulliver is trying to betray and dethrone him. Gulliver is the type that runs a pub and says 'righty-ho!' with great jauntiness. He gives himself out to be a retired naval commander but in fact was in the R.A.F. and grounded early on for L.M.F. – the dreaded citation: 'lack of moral fibre' (fervour?). At any rate Galen is presenting a pretty soft underbelly to him, and I fear the worst."

"I read some more of your drafts last night; it's queer stuff, some of it, and has a kind of bearing on what I have done. How shall I say it? You know full well that there is always something going on in the room next door and you often find yourself wondering what it might be. But it's never what you think. Your version of our book gives the presence of events, mine the absence, if I can put it like that."

Sutcliffe nodded somewhat gloomily. "Yes," he said,

"and it's because you really exist. I'm just a figment, living by proxy, turned on and off at will like a memory. I'm only as real as is necessary. My existence is contingent. Our books are linked without being interlocked, if you see."

"Hail!"

"Hail!"

"Be ye versions of one another, says the Bible!"

"Husband thy immortality, says Job."

Blanford gazed long and thoughtfully at his fiction and said, "I have given you a bad time, I know; that awful marriage, and all the sadness. But now at last we are both moving towards our apotheosis, you as a fat, sad oracle, me as a post-war crock with designs upon the Underworld only. No more love, no more apple-pie in the sky. Life will become an extended reverie – and of course a number of us must die. Don't forget it. You at least can't do the whole thing, you are limited to a fiction's dying. But the result can be moving or instructive or both. I shall be so glad to get you out of my system at last, my Old Man of the Sea!"

"What you mean is that at last this terrible but blessed war, which has prevented us from thinking about ourselves – or even *for* ourselves – is coming to a close and we are soon to be thrown back on our own resources. Winter quarters for the 10th Legion, and Iron Rations!"

"I am in love with Constance!" he suddenly blurted out like a schoolboy attacked with the squitters.

Sutcliffe looked quizzical and just a trifle ironic. "*Enfin!*" he said. "Something that was not in the script! Something unexpected! But it could be untrue, couldn't it? You yourself are fond of pointing out the self-deceptions of others . . ."

"To hell with you!" Blanford said, fully aware of the appropriateness of the oath. The fat man said, "You mistake me for Monsieur, doubtless?"

"Doubtless!"

Sutcliffe chuckled indulgently and wagged a reproachful finger at his fellow scribe. "You know that Affad is back, don't you?" Blanford did not. At that moment Cade knocked and entered on a note of interrogation. "You rang, sir?" Blanford looked up and shook his head. "No, Cade. I didn't." The valet looked puzzled and aggrieved. "Well, someone did ring," he insisted before turning away to leave the room. Blanford said, "Where is Affad, then, why hasn't he made some sign of life?" Sutcliffe, who was sharpening a pencil, shrugged his shoulders. "How should I know?" he said. "Since all the romantic convulsions I have hardly dared to mention him for fear of upsetting Constance."

"I think," said the irritated Blanford, "that we are all behaving like a gaggle of maiden aunts and the result will simply cocker up the girl's ego – already too swollen, in my humble opinion!" Sutcliffe looked at him with an ironic smile; "Hoity-toity," he said, "such vexation now! I think we must leave it to Affad now to reappear and set things to rights."

But it was the following day that Affad suddenly appeared in their midst during a mid-morning gathering in the old Bar de la Navigation – though the presence of Constance was quite a rarity: she was usually far freer in the evenings. Yet on this fine morning she had made a detour on foot in order to catch Sutcliffe with a message about Trash – and had been persuaded to stay and have a drink.

A car drew up in the street outside and suddenly with a heartleap – a desperate sense of total heed – she saw a familiar form merge up on the glass-fronted door and heard the bell tingle as he pushed it open. There stood Affad after what seemed several centuries, though it was only a matter of months. Her first impulse was to turn away, perhaps even to flee, but she converted it in characteristic fashion. Advancing upon him with a smile of welcome she caught him almost before he had entered the room and with a kiss she stuck a flower in his gun, so to speak, saying lightly, "Are we speaking to each other or not? I have forgotten." It sounded challenging and frivolous, and she all at once repented when she saw how thin and pale he looked, and how diffident. He said in a low voice, without any trace of affectation, "Of course. I *must* thank you – I don't know *how* as yet." And they allowed themselves to be submerged in the general conversation – for his sudden appearance had gained Affad a general welcome. Every one was anxious to know how he was and where he had been; and for a moment this somewhat boisterous greeting obliterated all other thoughts. He accepted a glass of beer and sat down beside her to drink it and to exchange banter with Toby and Ryder, while Blanford from his corner watched the face of Constance with a sardonic and yet resigned expression. The distress she had suffered with the separation – and particularly the confidences she had made to him as her best friend – had touched him to the heart and had increased this age-old attachment to her image. So much so that he almost forgot to be jealous of Affad whose friendship was equally dear: as if they all lived equidistant from each other. But now there was a whole jumble of misunderstandings between the lovers and as Constance sat there at his side, smiling and saying nothing, her heart continued to sink, for she could not imagine that such a breach would ever be mended, nor could she devise ways to heal the wound caused by this misunderstanding. How impossible men were, after all!

There were other factors also which added to her anxiety and undermined her self-confidence and poise. She cursed herself for the reaction, it was so childish: but he had hardly bestowed a glance upon her new hair-style. Did he perhaps dislike it? She caught a glimpse of it in the mirror and wondered if he thought it too loud, too feminist . . . But then at last when he deemed that his welcome had been well and truly lived he rose and said, "Constance, please may I talk to you for a few moments? I have things to tell and things to ask." He looked worn and pale and extremely uncertain of himself. ("Good!" she thought vindictively.)

They went out into the sunlight together and since the day promised to be so fine he suggested that they leave the car and walk along the lakeside, a suggestion to which she agreed.

Not without a certain trepidation, for she too seemed awkward and inhibited. But by dint of waiting and letting the rhythm of their walking chime he was at last able to collect his thoughts. "You know, you must know, you *must* have felt that I had decided not to speak to you again – and of course the reasons (I know they seem fatuous to you) were also plain. That is why when I came here I went to the lake house, intending to come into town as little as possible. But after I saw what you had done for the child – with your own science which I found so limited – I could not do otherwise than come and thank you for the tremendous gift." As they walked he put his arm about her shoulders. Then they turned to each other and embraced silently, clutching at each other like drowning people, and saying nothing more, it being so difficult to breathe. Near at hand was a public bench, and at last she broke away feeling half-strangled and choked with conflicting emotions. "Ouf!" she sat herself down, between tears and rueful laughter, and put her head in her hands. He came to her side and gently stroked her hair. (Perhaps after all he did not mind the new style?) As a matter of fact when they embraced he encountered the changed scent which for some reason he greeted with a sense of unease, almost of distaste. Yet he could not analyse why exactly!

"We are being punished for having done something so frivolous as to fall in love. Punished for being out of date." But all this was simply to fill in the gaps of the silence and to conceal his own overwhelming emotion – he had forgotten how much he sexually desired her. His fingers received waves of sex like electricity – he stopped short of reproaching himself! "We thought we were extremely clever and superior!"

"You are still so unsure of yourself!"

"Unsure of you, rather. I thought you realised more fully than you did how dangerous it might be to mess about with a machine you did not understand: a machine which was already launched upon a trajectory. One could lose an arm, an eye, a life. Perhaps I didn't explain very cleverly what we were up to – you thought of it as a vulgar suicide club, and of course being a spirited woman felt that it qualified my love for you – how *could* I both love you and passively subscribe to my own death from a hand unknown and at a time chosen by others? That is what you really felt, isn't it?"

"Yes." She said a little sullenly, "I suppose you could say that that is what a woman would feel. A deep disappointment in your manhood, really. I had the rather foolish notion of intervening, stealing the letter – I didn't quite make up my mind as to what I would do with it. At first I thought I would destroy it out of pure mischief and see what happened. No, I wasn't aware of any great danger because at bottom I did not take it very seriously – you had spoken of making a renouncement of the whole thing, pleading off . . . what was I to imagine? So I stole it while waiting to make up my mind and I put it in a book. Someone borrowed the book, a lunatic, and the precious document simply disappeared. My God, I'm so sorry for the thoughtlessness and the annoyance. We are trying to get it back, to find out what if anything the patient could have done with it."

"Your hands are cold." He sat down beside her on the bench and chafed them slowly as he talked. "I am as much to blame as you are, not for the letter, but for not explaining better what stood between us, and what you would have to accept in order to go on loving me. Yes, I did think of going back and attempting a renunciation, but really I knew it was hopeless. The minute I left your side I knew it was really out. I simply could not do it – it compromised the whole mechanics of the movement and what it had set out to do. I was a traitor!"

"Traitor!" she echoed ironically, and he pressed her hand, saying, "Yes. Yes. I know you think it schoolboyish, but there is a man behind me and a man before, I am part of a chain, a link. Our ambitions in a mad sort of way are scientific in the most exact sense of that misused word. We are setting up a chain-reaction which we believe could counter the laws of entropy – the irreversibility of process leading always to death, dispersal, disaggregation . . . Of course it is wildly ambitious. But, you see, it isn't just a romantic appetite for death as such . . ." He stared at her fixedly for a moment and then sighed, saying, "My God! I think you are beginning to understand. I was afraid you wouldn't – for after all it makes part and parcel of our loving: fucking is just the cement which binds together the double image we present to reality when an orgasm is shared, is reciprocally *breathed.* What does old Max tell you – surely something like that, no?"

"Yes. I was thinking of him."

"The man behind me represents the past and the man in front the future. In between those two poles I can say that I exist, only there, only in that *Now*. And in the duration I am experiencing I exist also in you, and you in me – *s'il vous plaît!*"

She was so happy that there would have been no point in being insincere and continuing to resist his warmth – though of course the brute badly needed punishing . . . "In spite of my misgivings I surrender. I am only sorry about my unpardonable intervention. But is it *all* that necessary to know the hour and the day?"

"In a sense, yes. To set one's affairs in order is only a secondary reason. But to accept the death transition profoundly is important because you pass the message on down the grapevine. What do you think societies and associations were created for? Reservoirs of energy and thought, dynamos, if you like."

"I see."

"So I feel that without that knowledge I am passing on a feeble signal. Like a dirty spark plug!" He put his arm in hers and said, "God! I am so happy I think I am going to faint!"

"Don't do that! Let me cook you some lunch. You are just faint from all your Egyptian excesses. But seriously – you have got very thin. Why?"

"I've been in the desert such a lot: one can't eat in the heat. Also I thought I had lost your respect. It was pretty bad, it made me realise that you were really a lovemate and that anyone else was out of the question – it would diminish what we had discovered in such an accidental way! I don't want to give you a swollen head so I won't go on. Anyway, it must be self-evident. What I really wanted to do was to father a child on you – by one act of perfect mutual attention: in a single yoga-breath, as you would say. Like you blow a smoke-ring, perfect and self-sustaining. Constance, why don't you shut me up?" But it was honey to her!

And there was only one way to do that and they sat and embraced so passionately that they received the curious or amused glances of the passers-by. Then at long last she proposed that they should walk back to her flat, but he had to sit still for a moment for he was in no state to stand up and walk – which amused her vastly. "Just think of ice-cream," she said, "and it will be all right!" But it was some moments before they resumed their walk. How glorious the sunlight seemed; they made a detour through the public gardens where preparations were almost complete for a local *fête votive*. Some of the stalls were already in place selling their fragile carnival wares, toys and ribbons and celluloid propellers and dolls for the children. They walked with their little fingers linked. She said to herself,

"It feels marvellous to be loved from top to toe, not an inch of you free from the honey." At a bar they ordered a bottle of cheap champagne and drunk it as if it were nectar. That is the terrible thing, she thought, love is really a state of mania!

From a medical point of view it was practically certifiable. She remembered him saying once, long ago, "Constance! Let's fall in love and create a disappointment of children!" And simultaneously she recalled Max telling her that "Every girl's a one-man girl, and every man too. Hence the trouble, for just anybody won't do – it's gotta be the him and the her of the fairy tale. Humans were born to live in couples like wild doves or cobras. But then we went and lost periodicity, meat-eating came in with the taste of blood: then sugar, salt, alcohol followed and we lost our hold on the infinite!" She wondered what Max would think of Affad's gnostic beliefs and obligations. Not so much perhaps, for the true yogi knew the hour of his death, and did not need artificial reminders in order to render it a conscious act.

"What are you thinking so sadly?" he asked.

"Nothing specially sad; just that time is passing; it has become doubly valuable since all this talk about death. Which is anyway impertinent and silly – trying to pre-empt reality when destiny may well be preparing to make an end of us in the next five minutes. We could be run over by a taxi."

"You are right; we will certainly pay for all these fine sentiments! God, though, it's marvellous to see you again, feeling all signals register and echo! The strategies of nature may be boundless but *this* thing puts them under the burning-glass."

"I loathe high-minded people like ourselves. We are just the type I can't stand."

"I know. And all this self-caressing sort of talk ruins fucking. Why don't we shut up and get on with it? I feel quite anorexic – sexanorexic. If you got into my bed I would be seized by paralysis. I would just dribble and swoon. Narcissus beware!"

They reached her flat and mounted the stairs arm-in-arm, still uplifted to the point of subversion by the bad champagne they had drunk; but also now a little afraid, a little withdrawn, because of the coming shock of their first encounter for so long. He looked particularly scared. The flat was spotless, the cleaning woman had been; and in leaving she had drawn the curtains so that they wandered into a half-darkened room. And just stood, quietly breathing, and regarding each other with anxiety, and at the same time so out of their depth.

"Sebastian!" she whispered, more to herself than to him, but he caught the name and took her hands, drawing her softly through the half-opened door towards the familiar cherished bed, reflected three ways by the tall mirrors, taking the hushed light of the window upon their bright skins.

The lovers, she was thinking, belonged to an endangered species and were in need of protection; should perhaps be kept on reservations like specimens of forgotten and outmoded physical strains, wild game? But was there any happiness which was the equal of this? To be blissed-out by the kisses of the correct partner, to make love and fade? Not to squander but to husband – a perilous game, really, for it was changing even while one was in the act of experiencing it. Yet there were so many people, perhaps the most, who arrived at the end of a life of limited usefulness to find the doors of this kind of happiness bolted and barred against them through no fault of their own – just scurvy luck.

Their clothes rustled and fell in a heap like a drift, and slowly, hesitantly they enfolded each other and drifted into the warm bed, to lie for a while breathing shakily, like freshly severed twins. So conscious also that kiss by kiss they would be winding steadily down into the grave. He was remembering some words from a letter: "Nothing can be added or subtracted from what exists, yet inside this wholeness endless change and permutation is possible with the same elements." Her teeth sank into his lips, he felt the sweet galbe of her flanks and arching back.

And yet, for all the tension, at the heart of their exchanges was a calm sensuality of understanding such as only those lucky enough to feel married in the tantric fashion experience. They were squarely each to each with no fictions of lust needed to ignite them. Embraces were woven like a tissue.

But because he had lost weight she took pity on him and hunted out chocolate from the kitchen – coaxing him with it to sweeten his drowsy kisses; and since he seemed the weaker today she took the dominant role, excited to drain him of every last desire by the authority of her splendid body. She feasted on his flesh and he let her go – though he was only shamming, saving his strength. And as soon as her passion subsided a little he suddenly turned her on her back like a turtle and entered her on a wave of renewal – a conqueror in his turn, but a welcomed one. All his strength had come back in a rush, as if from nowhere. But he knew that she had summoned it, had conjured it up. At last they lay entangled in each other like wrestlers, but immobile, and still mouth to mouth in a pool of ghostly sweat: and as proud of each other as lions, though meek as toys!

The telephone rang in its muted fashion, and she raised her head in drowsy dismay: "What a fool I am! I forgot to turn it off!" She was reluctant to unwind this matchless embrace for a mere professional call from Schwarz or someone. She hung back and hesitated, hoping that the invisible caller might suppose her absent and hang up; but no. The instrument went on and on insisting, and at last she crawled from bed and groped her sleepy way to the salon – only to find that as she picked up the instrument and spoke into it, it went quietly dead on her. She had just time to say "Hullo" twice before Mnemidis (for it was he) replaced the receiver with a quiet smile, having recognised her voice as that of his doctor and tormentor. So she was, after all, at home and not absent on duty as Schwarz had suggested! It was really wonderful how things fell out without any special interference on his part: they just fell into the shape dictated by his desire! Meanwhile an irritated Constance hovered above the phone, wondering whether to switch it off or not – her professional conscience reproached her for the wish. On the phone pad was a phrase which Max had given her, a quotation from a philosopher. She read it drowsily as she debated within herself the rights and wrongs of pushing the switch of the phone. "Everything is conquered by submission, even submission itself, even as matter is conquered by entropy, and truth by its opposite. Even entropy, so apparently absolute in its operation, is capable, if left to itself, of conversion into a regenerative form. The phoenix is no myth!"

Ouf! Her bones felt full to overflowing with electricity; she was outraged to find him snugly asleep instead of awaiting her! That was men for you! Yet to tell the truth she herself was not far off the same state, and enfolding him in her arms once more she fell quietly asleep, pacing him with her heartbeats! He could not guess how long this state of felicity had lasted when at last he awoke to find her lying wide-eyed and silent beside him. "What is it?" he whispered. "Did I wake you, did I snore?" But she shook her head and whispered back, "I was woken by an idea, a marvellous idea, and quite realisable unless you have any special plans for spending your time. Why don't we go away together for a few months, to really discover each other – supposing you *have* a few months at your disposal? Why waste the precious day? I have accumulated a lot of leave. Provence is cleared of Germans. I have an old house which we could open up, very primitive but comfortable and in a beautiful corner near Avignon . . ."

"How funny," he said, "for I was going to suggest something like that; I even borrowed Galen's house for the occasion. Yes, we shouldn't sit about waiting for time to catch up with us. We should act boldly like people with forever in their pockets. Perhaps this time I might actually . . ." But she covered his mouth with her hand.

She dared not think of becoming pregnant by him, with so many outstanding issues confronting their love. No, they must advance a step at a time, like blind people tapping a way with their white sticks. Paradoxically her very elation was terrifying. With him she might even dare to utter the words "*Je t'aime!*" which had always represented to her a wholly unrealisable territory of the feelings, of the heart. But then everyone alive is waiting for this experience, with impatience and with despair. Everyone alive!

They slept again, then woke, and drowsed their way slowly towards the late afternoon when the unexpected fever awoke in him – an onslaught so sudden that the symptoms for her seemed instantly recognisable as a rogue attack of malaria. But at first she was startled at its violent onset, to see him jumping and shivering with such violence, while he could hardly speak, his teeth chattered so in his head. "I brought it back from the desert – they have been planting rice like fools, and now you get anopheles right up to the gates of Alexandria!" But if his temperature had gone through the ceiling his pulse had sunk through the floor. He hovered now on the very edges of consciousness, but without undue alarm, for he knew that it would pass. Only with fury and self-disgust, for he was dying to make love to her again. And he had broken out into a torment of sweat. She found a thick towelling dressing-gown with a hood – indeed, they had stolen it from the hotel he had last occupied when in Geneva. An ideal thing for such a state, though it took quite an effort to get him into it, for he almost could not stand because of these paroxysms of trembling. He almost dropped on all-fours under the attacks. The sudden change was quite alarming, for he was ashen-white and all curled up. Malignant malaria is well known for its sudden paroxysms of fever which arrive or depart with incredible suddenness. But here was a temporary end of their love-making: he would simply have to sweat his way through the bout until the fever left him. She heaped him with blankets while he obediently turned his face to the wall and quivered his way into a half-sleep with a temperature so high that he was all but delirious. She did not even take his temperature in order not to alarm herself! Of course there were drugs which, administered in the night, might help to bring the fever down on the morrow. But of course he would be as limp as a cat afterwards . . . Damn!

Damn also because the telephone rang at that moment, and this time it was the voice of Schwarz, sounding preter-naturally grave, as if he were trying to master a concern or an anxiety. "I have been trying to reach you everywhere to tell you that your pet patient has broken out and escaped. Yes, Mnemidis!"

She thought for a long moment and then said, "Isn't our security foolproof? What about Pierre?" Schwarz replied, "He has stabbed him quite severely with a carving knife from the kitchens. But he has clearly got away because he made a phone call to his doctor friend from Alexandria and was most excited by their news. You know they were trying to take him back home? Well, they have succeeded in getting a *laisser-passer* for him from the Swiss, and there is nothing to prevent him just meeting them and being airlifted in a private plane – which is standing by at the airport. That is why I am not proposing to get unduly alarmed by the break-out; but I have moved into a hotel and asked a carpenter to change the locks on my flat. I think you should do the same. Until we get the all clear. The Alexandrian doctor has promised to signal me when he is safely in their custody so that they can escort him back to Cairo. What a bore it is! I hope you are feeling a bit chastened for having insisted on keeping him under treatment? No? Well, you should. At any rate, Constance, don't take any chances. For the moment he is somewhere in town, and nobody knows exactly where. So . . . Be on the *qui-vive* please, will you?"

"Very well," she said, though without conviction.

SIX

The Dying Fall

MNEMIDIS WAS MAKING THE MOST OF HIS FREEDOM, HE was filled with elation at the excellence of his disguise and the anonymity it conferred, though he looked a somewhat able-bodied nun. But he revelled in the unfamiliar beauties of the old town. As for the *fête votive*, it was so very touching and innocent that he was almost compelled to brush away a tear. It was very affecting. He laughed heartily and sincerely at the vastly correct jokes, careful not to boom, however. The squeaky exchanges of Punch and Judy and the rapt enthusiasm of the children filled him with an emotion close to dread. Once in Cairo long ago a little child had come to him, perhaps ten years old, doubtless a Bedouin and lost in the city . . . he had a fit of harsh coughing. It was time to be moving on. He was waiting for the evening to arrive but he had not as yet actually located the situation of the apartment he planned to visit. But there was a most convenient tourist map of the city outside the gardens at the bus stop. There was also a list of the principal avenues and a marker to help find one. He spent a long moment doing so and verifying his own position vis-à-vis the street in question. He had all the time in the world. He had already been astute enough to phone to the hotel of his two Cairo associates, and the doctor had given him the good news of his successful *démarches*, of the Swiss *laisser-passer*, and of the private plane waiting for him. Mnemidis was overjoyed, but asked for a little time before joining his associates; he had something to do in the town first, but he thought that it might be possible to meet them at the airport late in the evening, say at dinner time or just after . . . All this in a fine colloquial Arabic with its reassuring gutturals. "Above all," said the doctor, "do not commit any indiscretions, for you will be locked up for good, and we will never be able to release you. Take care!" Mnemidis chuckled and said that he would take care.

But there was time enough in hand, so having fixed a rendezvous at the airport at nine with the hope of a midnight departure, he left all the details to his friend, asking only that he might be met with a parcel containing a change of clothes, male clothes. He did not expatiate upon his present disguise because at bottom he trusted nobody. But his freedom and the secrecy of his whereabouts put him in a strong position to dictate his own terms. All the rest was up to him. He decided, since the afternoon was agreeably warm, to walk slowly across Geneva, and this he did, humming happily under his breath.

His route took him across the seedier parts of the old town, the poorer quarters, full of *maisons closes* and oriental cafés and moribund hotels; not to speak of the blue cinemas playing pornographic films. The one thing the war had not changed or debased was pornography; if anything, far from reducing it, it had caused an efflorescence, an increase. So necessary is it for the scared human ego to belittle a force which it recognises as being incalculably stronger than itself—the only really uncontrollable force man knows: for even if repressed it bursts out in symbolism, violence, dreaming, madness . . . Mnemidis slackened his pace in order to take in the whole scene with a just pleasure. There were a few sleazy whores already on the street, and the cinemas were rich in promise. He lingered at the entrance looking at the stills, attracting a number of curious and amused looks for he was still in his nun's garb. What marvellous titles the films had, expressing the age-old wishes and dreams of poor man, revealing him in all his frailty. He chuckled with an ape-like sophistication!

In the rue Delabre there was *Queue de Beton* or *The Concrete Prick*; further down *Plein Le Cul* or *A Cuntfull* and further on *Les Enculées* or *The Buggered.* It was absolutely delicious! He tore himself away with difficulty. It was with deep regret, however, for he simply longed to pass away an hour or so watching the antics of a blue film – it sharpened his intelligence. In it he felt the profound succulence of abused flesh. Even to think of it gave him hot flushes. However, he could hardly enter such a place in his present garb, and of course he did not wish to draw too much close attention to himself. But how reassuring it was to think that if all went well – and why should it not? – he would be leaving the country of his unjust captivity that very night! It elated him beyond measure, and he almost made the mistake of lighting a cigarette, for he had bought a packet. But he resisted the impulse successfully. He wandered past the cinemas and along the silent avenue leading to the park. He was not far off now, and he was filled with a silent felicity for he knew that luck would be with him in this just enterprise.

The mad must be people without selves: their whole investment is in the other, the object. They are ruled by the forces of total uncertainty. At this point Mnemidis did not know, with one half of his brain, what he might do under the promptings of the other half. A delicious uncertainty!

Like the greatest of mystics he had arrived at an unconscious understanding of nature as something which exists in a state of total *disponibilité*, of indeterminacy, of *hovering*! He was the joker in the pack, he was equally ripe for black mischief or the felicity of pure godhead. It was all according to how the dice fell, the wheel spun. Moreover he recognised that nature itself was completely indifferent to the outcome – to human bliss or pain. He felt only the electrical discharge of impulse throbbing in his body, like the engine of a ship, driving him onwards to the harbour of his realisation, a mystic of crime!

There is no therapy for reason, any more than for original sin. Yet sometimes even now he almost awoke from this mood, shook himself like a dog, wondering of a sudden if some small element had not worked loose somewhere in his inner thinking ... some tiny link. But he could not bear the wave of oppression and mistrust which followed in the wake of this sentiment and he closed his mind upon it like a steel door. His mouth set in a grim line. And now here he was in the street he had been seeking, standing before the very house he proposed to visit, utterly sure that everything had been planned for him, so that he might execute an exemplary punishment in the form of a farewell to Swiss medicine. And, by goodness, the door was ajar into the hall, for Constance had slipped out to the nearest pharmacy in search of a febrifuge for her fever-bound lover. She would not be gone very long. Hence she left the flat door ajar. Mnemidis saw with deep satisfaction the black shadow of the nun like some allegorical bat mount the stairs with a kind of Luciferian deliberation – as if she had been summoned to read a service for the sick or to hear the confession of someone *in extremis*. He chuckled to find that the flat door was also open. He entered and stood for a long moment looking about him, as if to memorise the geography of the place; but in fact he was simply listening to his own heartbeats and soliciting his soul, asking himself what he should do next. He heard the faint stirring of the bed in the next room and boldly opened the door – also ajar! His heart swelled up in triumph for there was a figure in the bed, covered from head to foot in a towelling dressing-gown with a hood drawn right over the head. Its face was turned to the wall, away from him, and from the whispering and trembling he at once guessed that she must be in a high fever, practically a delirium. But it was mysterious that she should be here all alone, lying ill in this darkened room. Perhaps there was someone else in the flat? With great swiftness now he explored all the other rooms, and then subsided with relief, for there was not a soul. What a perfect situation. "I told you so!" he said to himself under his breath, and breathing deeply like a voluptuary he advanced towards his victim.

It was lucky also that he had to deal with this inert and passive form and not a target presenting more difficulties – having to struggle, use force or ruse. No, the white form lay before him as if upon a slab, waiting to be operated on; in the beautiful simplicity of the whole business he felt he could read the handwriting of higher providence. Yes, this was how it had to be! And poising himself with profound concentration he put one hand upon the shoulder of the figure and completed his work with such speed and dexterity that he quite surprised himself. There was no cry, no groan, no sudden spasm. Just a deep sigh, as if of repletion, and a small gulp – a mere whiff of sound. With knives so preternaturally sharp it was hardly necessary to thrust with force, nevertheless he took no chances and gave of his best. *Consummatum est!* A whole mass of gloom-laden preoccupation seemed at once to fall from his shoulders. It was as if his conscience had voided itself like a sack. He almost cheered in his elation. But he wiped the weapons most carefully upon the silent shoulder of the corpse and then crossed the room on tiptoe. In the salon was a writing desk with a framed photo of his tormentor looking particularly pretty and intellectual. He stared at it for a long time, smiling grimly with a satisfied air. It was here, under this picture, that he at last placed the missing letter which she had been kicking up so much fuss about during recent weeks. Once when young he had been apprenticed to a conjuror and had retained a few of the skills he learned – making things appear and disappear with professional skill. It had not been difficult to do this with the letter. But now he was going to surrender it – like a parting snub!

He withdrew as silently as he had entered, closing the flat door behind him with a slight click – indeed this is what puzzled Constance on her return a quarter of an hour later: finding the flat door shut. It was vexatious for she had no key and she did not want to tap and awaken her patient. She returned downstairs and rang for the concierge who had a master key which she loaned her. She entered at last to stand in startled surprise at the open door of the bedroom, her arms full of medicines. But almost at once the unnatural silence and inertness of the figure on the bed struck a chill of premonitory alarm in her. And peering as she advanced she saw the bloodstains on the sheet and shoulder of the wrap. She held her breath and let drop the package she held. She called his name once, then twice on an even sharper note of interrogation, alarmed by the stillness. One thin hand stuck out of the wrap, contracted up now in death like the claw of a dead bird. She fell upon the pulse for a long moment, ferociously concentrated with total attention. Then with a gasp she drew back the sheet and began to unwrap the silent parcel, letting out a wail of anguish as the reality of the affair came rushing at her, engulfing every feeling. How could it be real, and as she drew back the wrappings strange jumbled thoughts and memories contended in her head with her concentration upon the terrible reality of the situation – the wounds! Once someone had told of unwrapping an Egyptian mummy to get at the precious eatable flesh which is the soul-nourishment of the gnostic – and noticing that it had been stabbed *through* the wrappings, that is to say after its death. Now who would fall upon and stab a a body already dead and parcelled up for the grave? The mystery remained! Yes, it was Affad who had told her. And now this white towelling dressing-gown was the very same into which she had bled so copiously upon her first sexual encounter with him. They had stolen it from his hotel as a kind of lover's talisman. When she had uncovered his body and made quite sure she started to faint; she had just enough presence of mind to dial the emergency code, four-number four-ambulance which might come to her aid. But it was someone else's voice it seemed that told the operator to summon

Schwarz to her side. Then she fainted away. And so they found her.

Half-falling, half-subsiding upon the bed beside him she was possessed of a private stupefaction which would soon (like rings widening in water from a thrown stone) become public – or at any rate more public, for this sudden abrupt disappearance from the scene of Affad seemed as unbelievable to everyone as it seemed incomprehensible to her. But by now she was on the way to recognising the handiwork of her most interesting patient. She was stunned and bemused into an incoherence of mind which alarmed Schwarz when he at last arrived, though he did not go as far as opening the black leather suitcase which housed his drugs. It seemed more appropriate that she should cry, should give public expression to her shock – not just sit bereft and stunned and tearless in a chair with blood all over her skirt. Gazing in puzzled silence at his face with its now gigantic reserve, its depth and weight. All the memoranda of past conversations swarmed over her, invaded every corner of her apprehension. She was absent-minded, tongue-tied, shocked into aphasia almost. She said to herself something like, "So the future has arrived! Life will be no longer a waste of breath!" But the dazzling fact of his death still blinded her – like stepping in front of a firing squad and refusing the bandage. Was the death of a heart impossible to accept – it had, after all, been part of the original contract? How deafening was the silence in which they must now communicate with each other!

Yet the mechanical part of reality still held together like a stage-setting defying an earthquake – once the ambulance with its duty-doctor and team arrived, followed very shortly by her colleague, a rather trembly version of Schwarz. His gestures also were part of the whole stereotype, only they were more efficacious for he knew the flat; and from the cocktail cabinet under the window he extracted the bottle of vodka. The fiery dose he poured out for her made her hesitate; but then she drained the glass and the liquid poured into her like fuel into a furnace bringing heat without joy, without surcease. Nevertheless.

The intern was making a gingerly examination of the wounds before permitting the parcelling up of the body for the stretcher. "Surprisingly little blood," he said in a whisper almost, as if talking to himself. "Considering . . ."

Considering what, she wondered? Then of course she saw that one of the crew had found a knife which seemed to correspond to the victim's wounds. It was wrapped up carefully in newspaper for the coroner. It was another of Mnemidis' little offerings. "Finish your drink," said Schwarz sternly, "and sit quiet for a moment." He felt suddenly very angry with her, irrationally angry. He could have smacked her face. This is what came of meddling with other people's destiny – he did not say it aloud, but that is what he felt. Constance said, "He told me he was leaving his body to the hospital. He said, 'I like to think that I shall end up in chunks like a pineapple; after all, I was built up that way on the assembly line!' Easy to say." Schwarz did not at all like the note of her laugh at this awkward pleasantry so he sat down and put his arm about her shoulders.

There was some documentation to be completed and here Schwarz was master; he filled in the forms with expert swiftness, talking all the while to the intern. Meanwhile the stretcher was raised and borne away to the waiting ambulance and the flat door closed. The two doctors shook hands; Schwarz had already sketched in the context of the murder. Later on, the next day, he would find a message on his telephone recorder from the Egyptian doctor which would tell him that everything had worked perfectly, and Mnemidis had duly arrived at the airport, ready to embark for Cairo. There was nothing to be done in effect. What would have been the point in trying to get the madman back? He would be judged unfit to plead and locked up once more – to what end?

SEVEN

Other Dimensions Surprised

"OF COURSE THERE MUST BE A SERVICE," SAID THE Prince with unaccustomed testiness. "Forms must be observed as he would have wished." She shook her head. "I think *he* would have been indifferent–however, we shall do what you wish."

"It's easy to talk idly," said the Prince snappily, "but quite another to deal with a reality like this." His eyes filled with tears, and seeing that, so did hers. "You can imagine how guilty I feel," she said, almost whispering, and he took her hand to press it sympathetically. He felt that her heart was still only adolescent, still burning to grow up: and now this dire calamity stood in the way of its natural evolution towards maturity. "There's another thing," he said. "You will be quite surprised by the number of people who will be touched by this sudden loss. I think the chapel on the lake will be suitable for becoming a *chapelle ardente*, and we must publish the fact in the press perhaps–don't you think?" She was too tired to think. Things were resolving themselves without her intervention. She felt that her mind had gone numb. The little chapel in question was a small architectural vestige standing among mulberry trees on the water almost. It was part of the grandmother's property. It had not even been ordained for services–indeed had never been used except once for a christening. It would do admirably. But she was unprepared for the number of people who put in an appearance at the ceremony itself, and for the feeling which was generated by the sight of his quiet face, pale now and somewhat drawn, in the big gondola-shaped coffin in which he had been laid. There were so many humble people like office-messengers and filing-clerks and typists, some of whom shed tears of real grief at the sight! One had quite forgotten that he had played a part in the public life of the town, and of the Red Cross; then of course her immediate friends, Sutcliffe wearing a tie, Blanford in his chair, Toby, the Prince, and of course Schwarz – all with their attention oriented towards the Pole Star of his death, of his silence. But he himself seemed detached, almost as if he were listening to distant music – perhaps he was? Fragments of old conversations floated backwards through her mind, as when she once said, "Damn it, I believe that I really do love you!" And he had replied ruefully, "It comes with practice I am sure – but will we have time?" Prophetic question!

Nor had it been difficult to find a Coptic priest who, together with his youthful novice, chanted the seemingly interminable Egyptian service of the dead, their thin, gnat-like tones stirring quaint echoes among the cobwebbed arches of the upper chapel. Geneva is the capital of cults and movements. Priests of all the denominations abound. The ceremony was at once exotic and fanciful and at the same time highly conventional owing to the soberly clad group of civil servants in their bourgeois clothing.

She had spent the afternoon lying across the foot of Blanford's bed; when she arrived at the clinic he was already in the know, for Schwarz had telephoned him. Constance simply marched into the room and said, "Please, Aubrey, I don't want to talk about it, indeed about anything. Can I just lie here for a few minutes?" She placed her hand in his and gradually swam out into a deep oceanic sleep which was to last a couple of hours. Blanford said nothing – what was there to say? But he felt the stirring of his old passion for the girl and his heart drew encouragement from the soft pressure of her hand in his. He felt that one day she must come to love him. It was something that was to be forged by time and circumstance; it could not be rushed! But it was in the final analysis ineluctable.

He was terribly happy and moved by the presentiment, by the promise of a future full of happiness. How can one feel so sure, though? And was it wise to encourage such optimism? She lay at his feet sleeping like a young lioness.

But he too was a prey to new conflicts centring around guilt, for it had suddenly dawned on him that quite possibly he had hated Affad without being fully aware of the fact. It was extraordinary how the news of his friend's death had brought him a sense, if not of elation, of peace and well-being, of fulfilment almost. He was too curious about the emotion to indulge in self-reproach – moreover, the whole thing was so unexpected. But it seemed unworthy of Constance to accommodate vulgar emotions like jealousy. ("Why *vulgar*?" he asked himself.) Was his love suffering from the blood-poisoning of over-refinement? Or was it just a coarse plebian growth like everyone's? He watched her sleeping face with attention as if he might perhaps read the answer on it, to master the secret which so far he had never expressed.

"Cet homme n'avait qu'à ouvrir les bras et elle venait sans efforts, sans attendre, elle venait à lui et ils s'aimaient, ils s'embrassaient . . ." Yes, he suddenly felt the quiet suppressed fury of Flaubert's jealousy and recognised it as his own. "A lui toutes les joies, toutes ses delices à lui . . ." For *him* all the joys, all the delights for *him*! "A lui cette femme toute entière," for him this woman entire, head, throat, breasts, body, her heart, her smiles, the two arms which enfolded him, *ses paroles d'amour*. A lui tout, à moi rien! He stirred her sleeping body softly with his foot, almost apologetically for what he deemed an ignoble line of thought. Ah! This power-house of human misery and ecstasy, the cunt! What Sutcliffe called "the great tuck-box of sex". How much thought, how much science would it need to control its ravages?

She spoke now without opening her eyes so that he could hardly tell whether she was awake or not. "Did you see what the little boy did?" Yes, he had seen. "Yes, I got quite a shock, a sort of shiver ran through me. I felt the significance of his decision, the weight of it. One simple decision like that alters the whole of a life. Am I romancing?" She gave a brief sob and fell silent.

What had happened was this: in the small chapel they had formed several different groups with the family servants and the grandmother (in all the splendour of her mourning costume – superb garments, for the Egyptians are best at mourning, it has always been so): she stood away to one side with the little boy beside her clad in his eternal sailor suit with its HMS *Milton* on the hat . . . while Constance stood far forward on the left so that she could watch the quiet face of her lover who seemed so inexplicably still. All of a sudden she heard the click of small heels on the stone flags and turning her head saw the boy leave the side of the old lady and walk with premeditated decisiveness across the whole width of the chapel to Constance's side. He did not look at her, but simply took her hand, and together they gazed in the looming shadows at the corpse in its gondola-like coffin. Meanwhile the service nagged onwards towards its benediction. The old lady released him with a half gesture of loving despair, spreading her hands as one who releases a cage-bird. Her eyes filled with tears but she was smiling. She realised the full significance of the act as indeed Constance did. It was hard not to tremble, but she managed an appearance of calm as she pressed the small hand which lay in hers.

It was a new role which seemed to be now presenting itself – the role of a mother, almost, which was part of the inheritance left her by Affad. It was the most unexpected of gifts, and one which she knew she must not refuse. At the end of the service she walked him back to his grandmother and handed him over without a word exchanged. But both had grasped the finality of the choice and both knew its value and its explicitness. The details could wait upon circumstance. The choice had been made and would be respected. She felt quite shaky with emotion as she joined the others in the garden outside the chapel where there was a little delay while people sought their cars. It was here that Cade came forward with a letter for Schwarz from some refugee centre.

Schwarz glanced at the printed superscription on the envelope and grumbled as he put the envelope away in his overcoat pocket, to read at leisure. "International Refugee Centre," he growled, scowling at Cade as he did so. The whole world was a refugee now that the war had at last ended. "How did you get hold of it?" he asked the servant suspiciously, and Cade replied with punctilio, in his sanctimonious whine, "It came in the Red Cross pouch, sir. As I knew I would see you here I brought it along to save time." The eternal messenger, bearer of the eternal telegram, the poisoned arrow! He was not at first to recognise the death sentence which the envelope contained.

Constance was woken from sleep by the appearance of yet another unexpected figure – a bronzed young giant of a man in uniform bearing the insignia of the Royal Medical Corps. Blanford greeted him with unusual warmth, almost as a long-lost brother. This was Drexel, the young doctor who had provided welcome medical first aid after the accident in the desert which had cost the life of Constance's first love. There was a spontaneous warmth and penetration in his regard, and a feeling of familiarity which immediately captivated her. "Bruce Drexel!" So that is who he was; and for his part the young man greeted her as if they had been childhood friends. He was eager to assess the merits of the extensive surgical repairs to Blanford's poor back and glanced through the dossier of the operations with keen interest. "You were right," said Aubrey, "to call it the restringing of an old *piano*, for that is exactly how it felt to me. But from a *piano à queue* they are gradually turning me into an upright again. There's a real promise that I may one day walk again, though I think that ballroom dancing won't ever be possible again. Never mind!"

"You are lucky to be here at all!" said Drexel reproachfully, and then stopped abruptly as he thought of the dead man, and recalled that he had been, after all, the husband of Constance. She rose to set her hair to rights in the pier glass while Drexel went on, though talking in a lower key, as if what he had to say might interest only Blanford. "You know something? Now the war is over, or almost over bar the shouting, the *ogres* are going to break free from diplomacy and return to Verfeuille once more – you remember the old dream we spoke of on the boat? The dream of *après la guerre*? Well, it is slowly coming true, I think. The old château is in pretty ruinous shape but we can fix that up slowly; and though it sounds romantic wouldn't you retire from the world if you could? Anyway I am going on down into Provence as an advance guard to take soundings for the two *ogres*. They think that by next spring we can put our plan into action for a permanent *ménage à trois* . . ." He hesitated, for Constance had turned back from the mirror and showed a disposition to re-enter the flow of the conversation once more. She sensed his reticence and hastened to say, "I know all about your plan, because Aubrey told me about it; and then I was delighted for you would be neighbours. But isn't it a little early as yet?"

"The Germans have gone, and things will slowly come back into true. The *ogres* propose to live very modestly on his pension while I have a tiny income of my own." He smiled and stretched and stood up. "Why don't you come down around Christmas and spend it with us? It's far enough off as yet to dream about."

It was curious how this casual suggestion set up an echo, a vibration in the consciousness of Constance. It was as if a door had opened somewhere in the further end of her thoughts and memories. Provence! She had been talking of going on leave ever since her return from the long gruelling spell she had spent there during the war. Why not inaugurate the peace there with a Christmas visit? "It sounds crazy," she said automatically, and the young man sighed and shrugged. "In any case," he said to Blanford, "your novel about the matter is finished: it only remains for you to see if we are going to live it according to your fiction or according to new fact, no?"

EIGHT

After the Fireworks

AND SO AT LAST THE CLOCKS RAN DOWN AND GENEVA, capital of human dissent, realised that it must formally fête the ending of the most murderous war in human history. Yet, despite everything, a war which had made her rich and confirmed her liberties as well as her boundaries. A particular day was agreed upon by the nations which would bear the brunt of the victory – celebrations seemed onerous in the prevailing exhaustion, yet it was appropriate that they should mark the event, however half-hearted, however reserved. A day of lamentation for humanity might have been nearer the mark, for to the work of Hitler and Stalin the Allies had added their own rider in the ominous word Yalta, thus completing the circle of doom which hovered over European history. Nevertheless a victory celebration had been accepted by all, and for something like a week the Swiss had been industriously transforming their lake frontage into a wilderness of medieval towers and gates and keeps which would supply a stage backcloth for the mammoth firework display which they had planned. And the new fad in town was to walk the lakeside after dinner each night to study the progress of the work, to watch the army of soldiers and civilians at work on the project, operating from a fleet of anchored pontoons over a length of several kilometres. Nothing had been seen like this since the Great Exhibition: nothing since Paris had transformed itself into fairyland for a spell just before the war broke out.

Constance walked the whole length of the lake with her colleague Schwarz several times a week now when returning from the clinic at night, or after dinner in town. It was always full of variety and interest, the slow progress of this one-dimensional project upon which the fires would burn, the lights flicker. Obscure scenes from medieval Swiss history were to be pictured here against the screen of fireworks, scenes which extolled the grandeurs of freedom and independence: perhaps, as Schwarz said ironically, also scenes which extolled banking and secret credit accounts . . . who can say? But their statutory walk was much enlivened by the occasion and they planned to dine together on Victory Night and to follow the progress of the display on the spot. "*Après la guerre!*" mused the old man as they progressed. "What can it mean? For war never really ends, like birth and death, perpetual motion . . . Before one can get to the end of one set of wishes or hopes along comes another. The options have changed! History makes a rightabout turn. I used to see much more sense in things when I was younger, consequently I was prepared to fight for them. Now it's all hollow, all empty, and I am ready to turn on the gas."

"Hark at you!" she said with indignation. "Only yesterday I heard you express a hope that Israel might emerge from the present chaos as a coherent entity. And now?" Schwarz depressed his cheeks and looked shamefaced. "It is true," he at last admitted. "I did say that I thought I saw an important role for Israel and hope she would come forth from the ruins. But Constance, the sense in which I spoke was far from political or geographical. For me the country is like a retort in which a vital experiment could and perhaps will be conducted. But this is in the domain of philosophy and religion – it has nothing to do with frontiers. I am hoping that something like the Principle Of Indeterminacy as posited by our physicists for reality will find its way into the religious values of the new state; I see you don't quite understand me so I won't labour the point. But I'm hoping for a materialism which is profoundly qualified by mysticism – a link between Epicurus and Pythagoras, so to speak. All right! All right! I think that our Hassidim have the creature by the tail and that they might help it to evolve. It would be a marvellous contribution to the future, for we can't continue with this worn-out materialism of ours, it leads us nowhere. And while we are eroding the Indian vision, drowning it in our technology, India is eroding ours, drowning Europe in all the vast meekness of pure insight!" He stopped.

"You mean the world is becoming one place?"

"Yes! It so obviously must if there is to be a future for humanity. Surely we can dream? Why should man be the only animal who knows better but always fares worse?"

This long, indeed interminable, argument of theirs wound its slow course across the weeks towards Victory Day which would mark the historic *point culminant* of things. Much of what he said was only imperfectly understood as yet by Constance and would come back to memory in the years to come – making her realise that with Schwarz she had received a sort of philosophic education invaluable for a doctor. But so often he was obscure, oracular, perhaps one could say almost 'vatic' in his vision, for he was after all Jewish in origin, with the broad stripe of mystical insight for which his race is known. The severe materialism of his apparent outlook was merely a façade to mask his other profounder preoccupations, as when he sighed, "To what extent have we the right to interfere with the principle of entropy, the cosmic submission which subsumes everything – the death-drift of the world?" It was the point at which East and West were still at loggerheads. Submission or intervention, which?

"No!" he went on. "The Nazi in the woodpile is a too strenuous orthodox Judaism which we can evolve and modify slowly into a richer complicity with nature. Absolutes spawn restrictive systems; but provisionals in their elasticity allow us to breathe."

He struck the ground defiantly with his stick and said, "I have a *right* to hope, after all!"

"That is what the Prince sometimes says!"

Schwarz snorted, for he was slightly jealous of the Prince, sensing how deeply Constance was attached to the little man. As a matter of fact the news from Egypt – which had followed the Prince, so to speak – was hardly reassuring, for all of a sudden the British authorities after years of quiet suspicion about the orientation of the gnostic groups had decided to investigate, and about twenty-five of the Prince's collaborators were at present under arrest pending an inquiry into their apparent political motives. It put him in a rage just to think of it! The shortsightedness, the imbecility, the waste of the whole thing! It really wasn't worth being pro-British when they behaved with such ill-judged stupidity! The whole storm in a tea-cup would end in nothing, for there was nothing secret and confidential to be discovered. One could already foresee the climb-down which would ensue, the apologies offered all round to the arrested club members! Goodness, what a fool that Brigadier M. was! But the realisation did little to soothe the ire of the Prince who felt that the whole operation had made a fool of him and of his pro-Ally sentiments.

Schwarz was thinking: "Larger than life or larger than death – which? The two ways, East and West!" What he wanted to do was to scale himself down to the size of his own death, which he could feel was not too far off now.

So they limped their way towards the point of victory, and the day dawned bright with church bells and religious processions – it was treated like a Holy Sunday and public holiday combined. But for the clinic this meant little difference – one cannot call a truce to the unhappiness of the insane just when one wishes, even to celebrate the end of a war. So it was evening before they found themselves at the Bavaria while outside in the grassy squares massed bands played and detachments of motorised troops marched and counter-marched to the music, waiting for the first pangs of white light from the anchored pontoons with their brilliant historic tableaux. There was ample time to dine, and under the influence of the red wine Schwarz waxed almost eloquent about firework displays he had seen in the past, in Vienna, in his student days; and once on a visit to Venice. How would this Geneva display compare in style and originality, he wondered?

But they were already walking across the park when the first maroons boomed out and the white effulgence coloured the dark air with sudden stabs of starkness, printing up the receding façades of the buildings like so many human faces and running with slippery unction from the lake surfaces tumbled by the night wind. Gradually, as they advanced, the whole axis of light slanted and the waterfront slowly took fire like a summer hillside, each section performing its duties with beauty and precision, so that the whole comprised a single jungle of impulses moving right and left, up and down, and printing out the city with every sulphurous stab, every explosion of light, every thirsty roar of rocket or meteor. And while this whole symphonic movement gathered weight the various historical tableaux began to print up, human figures began to move and bend and dance. (That afternoon the Prince had said to Constance: "Constance, you have suddenly started to walk like an old woman. It has got to stop! And you are letting your hair grow wild just like those pregnant girls who hope by doing so to conceive of a boy. Please pull yourself together. You must. Please use a little reason!") *Reason!* She repeated this to Schwarz who snorted with disdain at the word-choice. He was thinking to himself that reason made strange bed-fellows: how Socrates sought suicide like Jesus, but did not want to take the blame for the act. What a contrast to Buddha who thought that felicity and the rounded tummy were best!

They came upon a public telephone and Schwarz was impelled by a characteristic twinge of professional conscience to ring up the duty nurse at the clinic to find out if all the untoward banging and flaring had had a disturbing effect on the patients. But he refrained, he restrained the desire. He said, "The most haunting thing about human reality is that there is always something unexpected happening in the room next door about which one will only find out later on! Moreover it will prove surprising, totally unpredictable, and more often than not unpalatable!"

"Pessimist!"

"No, realist. Pragmatist!"

They advanced upon the starkly blazing water frontage, dazed by the variety of the scenes which were now being simultaneously enacted for their benefit – some from the late war, some from historic circumstances and events, some perhaps from wars to come, wars not as yet engendered in the human consciousness. The flames and scenes were striving to offer them a sort of summing-up of the years wasted in brutality and strife – in the hope that by closing the whole chapter a notion might be launched of some change of direction. Geneva was the capital of the moral reproach, the lost cause, the forlorn hope!

"When puberty came," said Schwarz grimly, "when I was around thirteen or so, a sudden terror took possession of me one day in church. I suddenly saw that everyone around me was abnormal, was ill, was mentally disturbed; I had realised that to be a Christian constituted being deranged in the purest sense of the term. The Quia Absurdam leaped at me, just like standing on the head of a rake. Moreover it was everywhere, all around me – the thirty-nine articles or the sixty-nine varieties of Heinz beans. I trembled and broke into a sweat just reciting the Creed after the parson – it seemed gibberish. Jesus was paranoid like Schmeister, driven mad by the strain of trying to break away from or assimilate the tenets of an orthodox Judaeo-Christianity. He had shared this fate with Nietzsche, the Christian syndrome. In the despair of my youth

I could see no hope of ever escaping it myself. What an experience for a sensitive youth! It marked me. Even now when I tell myself that I have escaped the worst I catch myself up abruptly and wonder . . ."

A dozen blazing swans whizzed heavenward spitting out tracer; sixteen pearls hissed after them trailing parabolas of flame. Constance thought, "We look to each other for nobility of conduct, for traces of the sublime. There isn't any such thing, no such hope. How did we get such ideas and wishes in the first place? They were bound to be disappointed!"

So they walked on like fellow-bondsmen shackled by the same ideas, swollen with the despair of hopes unsatisfied, of promises unfulfilled. What price their theories of health and disease when pitted against this sort of historic reality? She could feel the greyness creeping upon the outlook of her companion, could sense the cryptic sadness welling up in his mind. How senseless this huge and wasteful celebration seemed to her! It closed no door upon the past, it opened no door upon the future. It left them disconsolate and bereft – like beached ships. Abruptly – and without even waiting to see if she followed him or not – Schwarz turned aside into a café with a bar giving on to the lake gardens and angrily ordered double whiskies, but continuing the while to gaze at the display in all its distant splendour. Under his breath he was softly swearing – a habit Constance knew full well from the past. She put a hand on his arm to soothe him, and said, "Well, look who's here!" She had caught sight of Sutcliffe and Toby sitting in a far corner, apparently deep in conversation with Lord Galen whose manner suggested the deepest elation. Schwarz showed some reluctance to join them, for it was obvious that Sutcliffe had been at the bottle, and possibly Galen also; but their appearance was greeted with such a display of welcoming affability that it would have been churlish to turn one's back upon them without exchanging a word. So they advanced towards them, determined only to stay a few moments.

After suitable greetings they took their place at the table which was admirably disposed *vis-à-vis* the continuing firework display, and allowed Lord Galen to monopolise the conversation, which in a curious sort of way echoed their own preoccupations and doubts. It concerned the problems which they might anticipate in a post-war state of things. "I felt quite lost and thrown aside, I must confess," said Galen, "and I did not know which way to turn my talents. I knew that one day I must return to private enterprise. Then, like a signal from On High, I learned that Imhof was dead and that he had made a will in my favour – can you imagine? I had inherited those thousands of bidets which he had stored away in Dieppe in vast warehouses, just waiting to cross the Channel and convert the English, in order to help them to save water. Think, all through the war they had been laid up there, shrouded in anonymity, waiting. Suddenly I found I had inherited them. At first I was a bit panicky at the thought but finally my old business sense came to the rescue and I drafted a careful advertisement in *Exchange and Mart*. Sure enough – there is a market for everything if you can find it – I had an answer from the Society of Jesus, who proposed to export them to the Far East as part of a religious campaign. They found a way of printing 'Jesus Saves' on them in several languages, and away they went! I was left with a nice little sum after settling up the dues involved. I was able to consider leaving the ministry with all its insoluble problems. But of course civil life was also full of grave discouragements, I don't deny it. I decided that I should diversify my investments but I did not know quite how when . . . guess what . . . I got an idea from Cade, of *all* people, Aubrey's factotum. I heard him say to his master, 'Lord bless you, sir, the future will be just like a past. Nothing is going to change. Everyone is going to go on in the same old way, you will see.' It carried conviction, I suddenly realised that it was true. I saw that one should still invest in the old values, the old beliefs, with perfect security. So I decided to invest seriously in Marital Aids – for soon marriage would be booming again. I founded the Agency Vulva to sell a computer of that name – the only computer with a sex-life that is really life-like – it can twitch, throb, corybant at the pressing of a button. It is most exciting and is well on the way to building itself a world market. I owe all this to the insight of Cade!"

He gazed around him with fatuous self-satisfaction, swollen with an innocent conceit at these antics. Sutcliffe banged his glass on the table approvingly and said, "I appoint myself your advertising manager. I will write you slogans of utter irresistibility like . . . 'Bring splendour to your marriage with our hand-knitted french letters.' Or for the Swiss something a bit aphoristic like 'C'est le premier pas qui coûte quand c'est le premier coup qui part!'" Galen shuddered, but with gratitude. "For the moment," he said hastily, "we need nobody. Perhaps later."

A Swiss military band with a pedantic goose-step marched across the middle distance against a blazing wall of Catherine wheels pounding out the music of Souza. Schwarz went on quietly swearing, with resignation, almost with piety, oblivious to the restraining caress of Constance's hand upon his elbow. Soundlessly, one might say, inside all this triumphant noise. His lips moved, that was all.

"I do not see," said Toby with a judicial air which could not hide a certain insobriety, "that the future can resemble the past in any way. Thanks to science the world has come to an end, for the woman is free at last, though she remains bound to the wheel of generation; she is free to spread sterility at will. The balance of the sexes is beautifully disturbed." Galen looked both perplexed and alarmed. But Sutcliffe nodded approvingly and said, "Exactly what I have been telling Aubrey, to his intense discomfiture. He also hoped that things would go on in the same old way. I was forced to disabuse him. Soon we are going to have to collaborate on a terminal book, and it's important that we should see eye to eye, so that it will be written, like all good books, by the placental shadow, me! Actually if it is to be historically true it should be entitled WOMAN IN RUT AND MAN IN ROUT. And of course the secondary result of this confused situation will be an increasing impotence in the male – *un refus de partir, mourir un peu beaucoup quoi!* My basic genetic alibi, my cockstand, will go all anaesthetic." He gave a low moan on a theatrical note. All this was calculated to increase the distress of poor Schwarz. If Sutcliffe was to be believed, what hopes could one hold out for the future of medical practice – specially something as fragile and contestable as psychoanalysis? Moreover they were *joking* about such a situation – joking about tragedy! He rose unsteadily to his feet and gazed wildly about him as if he were seeking a weapon. For the appropriateness of the subject-matter to the specific night – the victory carnival after nearly a decade of war – made the whole context ironic in the extreme. Constance rose also in warm sympathy with her colleague's fury, and prepared to set sail with him despite the protests of the others. As they walked away from the braying and banging of the spectacle towards the shadows Schwarz filled in the picture in his own mind with bitter thrusts of thought: yes, after all, Sutcliffe was right. Semantics would replace philosophy, economic judaism democracy, sterility potency . . . and so on. There was no way round the omens. But at least he, Schwarz, refused to be flippant about the matter. He *cared*, he was *concerned*!

At last they came to the last depleted taxi rank and he turned to bid her goodnight, for she had elected to stay at her flat in town for the night. "I am sorry to have been so very subversive on Victory Night," he said ruefully, "but what is there left to hope for, eh?" They embraced and he gazed long and tenderly at her before turning aside – a look which would remain with her for years, for this was the last time she was to see Schwarz alive; a look which summarised the tenderness and professional zeal which linked them in the name of their defective science.

She stood gazing after the taxi, touched by a dawning premonition of something momentous about to happen, she knew not what!

NINE

End of the Road

"ATTENTION CONSTANCE," SCHWARZ HAD WRITTEN ON their common blackboard in violet chalk before copying the phrase again upon a sheet torn from his prescription pad; this latter leaf he propped against the dictaphone. It bore an arrow and an exclamation mark and indicated the pyramid of wax cones upon which he had imprinted the true story of his death, his suicide. It would have been sad if by some inadvertence they had been overlooked or cleaned of their story. The cones were sorted most carefully and numbered; it was possible to hear his description and exposition of the whole business in strict sequence. Schwarz had always had a mania for order–it seemed to him to confer a sort of secondary truthfulness. And in this particular case he had been anxious to present his decision as reasonable, the act as pardonable because quite logical. Nevertheless there was some guilt mixed up in the business, for he had felt the need to make a case for himself.

They had both always despised suicide!

And now what?

"Constance, my dear, I foresee that perhaps you may be a little shocked by my decision, but I did not take it lightly; it has matured slowly over a period of time, and has only come to a head during this week, after receiving the letter which you saw Cade hand me – a letter which contained strange news after so many years of silence. It told me that Lily had been found at last and still alive! Found among the dregs of Tolbach, the notorious camp for women, in Bavaria. At first of course my heart leaped up, as you can imagine, and a variety of conflicting and confused emotions filled it; but then the letter contained news which was disquieting rather than reassuring. She had lost her teeth and her hair, was suffering from malnutrition as well as experiencing moments of aphasic shock . . . My first impulse was to rush to her side, but when I phoned the units working on the problem the doctor in charge advised me to give them what he called "a breathing-space", for he did not want me to be too shocked by her condition. He needed time to feed and rest her up a little. He posted me some photographs taken at the camp, of those who had been still alive when the place was discovered. Lily was only one of many, but fortunately she had been sufficiently coherent to give an account of herself, and they had found her dossier in the camp files. But the photographs they enclosed were hair-raising in their fierceness – this bald and toothless old spider, worn to the skeleton with hunger – this was all that was left of Lily, the lovely Lily!

"Connie, you know just how deeply guilty I have always felt about her – about my cowardice in escaping from Vienna without her, and leaving her to the mercies of the Nazis – to almost certain death. There was no excuse, and I never *tried* to excuse this terrible failure of nerve. But I lived, as you know, bowed under the guilt of this act all through the war – even sometimes perversely hoping that she might never return to judge me – though I knew it was not in her nature to judge! But it was there, the guilt. And then at other times I thought of her possible return as a joyful event: it would give me a chance to make it all up to her, to repay her for all her sufferings . . . How skilfully we can untangle the delusions of others! Yet when it comes to one's own one is powerless not to believe in them, not to swallow our self-manufactured fictions!

"Of course I was impatient with myself. I tried to treat the situation in a masterful fashion; I took up the phone and implored the doctor to put me in touch with Lil, direct touch. He deplored the idea but agreed and gave me a time of day which would be suitable. But I was unprepared for the dry clicking of her voice with its shy pauses, its lapses of memory. It was like talking to a very old and half-mad baboon." (Here the terse narrative was caught up with a dry sob. After a long pause the grave measured voice of the old doctor resumed the thread of his story.)

"I was gradually coming to a new point of realisation about her; it was dawning on me that her return to me in this new form was something to be dreaded rather than wished for. For so many years the thought of her had acted upon me like a sharp reproach; but now she threatened to become something altogether more fierce still – a living, breathing reproach to the man who had been responsible for her distress, her imprisonment! I suddenly realised that I simply could not face such a *dénouement*. I was completely unable to swallow such an idea. Moreover this sudden violent revulsion was completely unforeseen. It surprised me as much as it shook me. What was to be done, then? To deny her once more? To repeat my original act of cowardice, apparently because she was in poor physical shape? Such a thing would be unthinkable, unpardonable! Then what alternatives were there? None. The only choice before me was either to submit or else to vanish from the scene. The solution printed itself on my mind with a simple finality which was incontrovertible! I could find not a shadow of doubt with which to counter its cold and absolute truth!" Schwarz paused for breath and one could hear the scratch of a match as he lit up a cigar and puffed reflectively before resuming his account.

"Naturally I envisaged something very swift and decisive, a bullet in the brain no less. And I unpacked the old revolver, broke it, and checked the shells. Then I put it carefully in my mouth like the well-briefed suicide I was – God knows, when I was a young intern I had helped clean up messes of this kind when on duty with a police ambulance. Memories came back to me as I sat there, feeling and looking foolish, with the icy barrel of the revolver pressing upon my soft palate. I knew of course that revolvers throw upwards as they fire and that one stood a fair chance of error if one fired it through the temple – one case I recalled had shot out his two eyes without inflicting upon himself the death he sought. The only foolproof way was to shoot upwards into the skull via the soft palate. This is what I proposed doing. What, then, was making me hesitate like this? Partly for company, and partly for encouragement I switched on the time-clock of the telephone and sat there listening to the disembodied voice repeating: 'At the fourth stroke it will be *exactly . . . Au quatrième toc il sera exactement . . .*' Don't smile! I just could not press that cold trigger. The seconds ran away like suds down a sink and there I sat, pistol in one hand and telephone in another, riveted. Another memory had surfaced – of a suicide who had actually done the trick classically, pistol in mouth. But the force of the explosion had removed the whole crown of his head like somebody's breakfast egg. An appalling mess for a young and shaky intern. I vomited violently as I worked at the cleaning up. Naturally I suddenly felt that I could not inflict this upon our own ambulance people. I rose and hunted out an old skull-cap of mine and a prayer shawl. Draped in these I resumed my vigil with the telephone and this time I stayed there obstinately, urging myself to show the necessary courage to complete the act. I had already sorted my papers, cheque books, identity kit, etc. so that Lily would have no problems when she re-entered civil life; I had even written her a cheerful note of welcome to my flat which she would soon own."

In the pauses of his discourse you could hear the puffs as he drew on his cigar and formulated what he wanted to say next. "Constance, I found I could not do it. A new cowardice had come to replace the old. I laid the pistol down – it is where you will find it. I am substituting a peaceable injection for it. It is less dramatic but just as efficacious. Goodbye, darling Constance."

His sighs expended themselves on the queer silence, and one was able to imagine what he was doing from the tinkle of the syringe against the ash-tray. He muttered a short prayer in his own language, but it was perfunctory and full of disdain for God in whom he believed only intermittently. Constance listened to all this sitting with the dead man at her side slumped at his work-desk. Then she called the Emergency Unit.

TEN

The End of an Epoch

It was late at night when the news of Schwarz's disappearance from the scene was telephoned to Constance who had celebrated a few days of leave by staying at her town flat, thus enabling herself to see her friends and even play a game of pool with Sutcliffe or Toby. The telephone cleared its throat and set up its rusty trill. She recognised the voice of the night-operator on the switchboard and heard with sinking heart the first ominous words which spelt the end of her leave. "Dr Schwarz has been taken ill. The Emergency Unit has been asking for you, doctor."

"What has happened?" she asked, but the line had already been switched, presumably in the direction of the emergency intern, for there followed a garble of clicks and voices and finally she heard the incongruous voice of the negro stretcher-bearer Emmanuel saying hoarsely, "*Mister Schwarz he dead.*"

"What?" she cried incredulously and the deep thrumming negro voice repeated the message more slowly. The import of the words sank into her – or rather she sank into them as one sinks into a quicksand. Surely there must be some mistake? "Give me the duty doctor," she said at last, sharply, and as Emmanuel faded she heard the voice of the emergency intern, old Gregory, take up the tale. "I think you had better come up here," he said. "I am afraid that the old boy has done himself in with an injection. At any rate he is sitting at his desk and his heart has stopped, and there is a syringe in the ash-tray beside him. But Constance, there are messages for you, and your name on the blackboard. I am reluctant to call anyone in until you have had a look at the scene for yourself. I can't really evaluate it, and I don't want to invoke the police at this stage. Anyway, perhaps you know why. Was he specially depressed?"

She gave a groan and a hollow laugh and said, "When is a psychiatrist not a psychiatrist? God, Gregory, are you sure that – I mean, perhaps if you massaged the heart?"

Gregory made a sound something like a groan and an exclamation of impatience. "We arrived much too late," he said. "He is becoming marbly already – I want your okay to uncurl him and spread him on the couch straight away. Otherwise the rigor will cause problems."

"Do so if you must," she said. "I'll be there as quickly as a taxi can bring me." But when she arrived they had as yet done nothing, dismayed by the scribble on the blackboard and the dictaphone tablets. Schwarz looked so normal and so homely that all at once she conquered her fear and her distaste, and was glad to sit down at his side and bend over to study the dossier which he had open before him and which he had been studying while he waited for the slow poison to uncoil, serpent-like in his veins, until it reached his heart. Gregory watched her for a while with sympathy and said, "Yes, she was probably the last person to see him alive, you will have to ask her. I have no doubt." Constance reflected, her face wore an expression of compassionate distaste. Gregory said, "She must have come here with her latest manuscript, and perhaps he told her why – unless you already know why." Constance stood up and said, "Now please leave me alone to listen to these wax tablets – give him the chance to tell me why himself, for that is clearly what they mean. Afterwards we can decide what is what, and reflect on the role of the police in this affair." Gregory nodded and lit a cigarette. "And this girl, Sylvie, who was quite a well-known writer – what of her? Was Schwarz in love with her?" Constance shook her head and said, "No, it's more complicated than that; I started to treat her myself – she is absolutely brilliant but schizophrenic. She fell in love with me, whatever that means, and the transfer went to hell, so that he was forced to take her back on to his roster, and to pretend that I had been sent far away, to India no less, in order to release her from her obsession with me. Such are the hazards of psychology!"

"Well, the best would be to leave you to examine all the data before coming to any conclusion about the matter; he was not one to cause mysteries. Besides, this whole dossier seems to consist of love-letters – presumably addressed to Schwarz."

"No," said Constance, "that is the trouble, they are always addressed to me. Schwarz's job is to post them to me in India – for he alone knows my address and will not reveal it to her – that is the cover-story which has enabled me to stand aside and switch her treatment to him. When I last heard she was enjoying a short remission from the malady – all the more cruel because she always remembers in sane periods what she did and thought when she was mad."

"I see."

"It is the saddest of all our cases because she is a woman of the greatest brilliance, her writings are quite marvellous in their poetry. I suppose I shall have to go and see her now and pretend that I am back from India. She will find herself quite bereft without him, her beloved doctor."

Gregory stood for a brief moment smoking a cigarette with a somewhat dispossessed air; then he said, "Well, I shall go back to Emergency and see what other calls have come in. If and when you want us just phone down."

"I will."

"Constance," he said with deep sympathy, for he knew how much the old man had meant to her, "Constance, bad luck my dear!" And in his awkward way he stooped to kiss her face. And now she was alone with the stooped figure of her oldest friend, suddenly overwhelmed by the surging memories of all they had shared together – memories now abbreviated by something as momentous yet trivial as a cardiac arrest. "Ah, my dear," she said under her breath, "why did you have to do the one thing you most despised?" She switched on the little recording machine and heard his voice etching itself upon the silence of the room as if in answer to her question. As he talked in that quiet, measured tone she examined the little phial from which he had drawn the fatal injection as well as the empty syringe leaning upon an ash-tray with two cigar-butts stubbed out in it. Everything had taken place quietly and quite circumspectly; the other suicide equipment, the revolver and the cap and prayer shawl were at the far end of the table.

The dossier was familiar, though since she had last seen it it had swollen in size with a number of new letters, all neatly typed carbons – presumably the originals had been sent to "India". Sylvie must have visited Schwarz and left it behind her. She recognised the dazzling alembicated prose which had so much impressed Aubrey. She had told him the history of Sylvie and shown him the early letters. She did not forget the occasion when she came upon him as he replaced them in the folder in which they lay. He looked up and his eyes were full of tears of admiration as he said, "Goodness, Constance, she has done it, she has done the trick, she has become it! Against this all my stuff is feebly derivative and merely talented! This is art, my dear, and not artifice." And he had begged to keep the file so that he could read and re-read the letters. He was much affected by the story of her life and of her unlucky illness as well as of her poetic obsession with Constance with whom she had fallen so deeply in love. Sitting beside her old friend and mentor, listening to his voice recounting his last hours, she thought over these incidents with a tremendous weariness. All of a sudden, within the space of a few months, reality had taken on a totally new colour; it was as if the world had suddenly aged around her, washing her up high and dry on to this shelf in time where she sat in a sort of trance listening to the voice of Schwarz and resting a hand upon the immobile shoulder. But she must have affected his centre of gravity for all of a sudden the corpse began to slide slowly towards her – she just had time to catch and steady it. Then she realised that it must after all be laid out and using all her strength she lifted and dragged it to the sofa.

It was something of an effort for her, although Schwarz was not a heavy man; but there was no evidence of the *rigor mortis* which Gregory had feared, and the corpse lay back with a supple easiness, though as she folded the arms upon the breast its eyes opened like the eyes of a doll and there was her friend gazing at her calmly and temperately from the realm of death! She drew her palm across the eyes to escape the disturbing vision. They closed and the whole face seemed to sink back into its new anonymity, a timeless contrition. She sat and listened to it expatiating upon the reasoning behind the act of departure, defending the self-annihilation which had deprived her of her oldest mentor, colleague and friend. From time to time she shook her head with reproachful resignation, or rose to change a waxen cone in the little machine. Inside herself the profound depression grew and grew, an enormous dismay which threw into meaninglessness her every activity, either intellectual or physical. The loss of Schwarz rose like a wall in her consciousness, almost as if he had been a husband, a mate, and not merely an intimate friend. Yet she was dry-eyed, composed, and kept on her features a sardonic expression suitable to such an ironic situation: but it was a pitiful boast and she knew it. The slow voice held her in thrall, the slow insidious argument unrolled itself in her mind, and she knew that reality had all but overwhelmed her, had shaken the basis of her inner composure. When at last it ended, the recording, she gave a sharp cry, as of a bird stricken by the hunter's shot, and turning back to Schwarz saw with disgust that his left eye had opened again. The other remained shut. It gave his face the faintest suggestion of slyness. It filled her with distaste. Impatiently she closed it once more with the palm of her hand, and then pressed down on both lids at once for half a minute to make them stay shut.

This time they stayed shut. She found a blanket and drew it over him. Then she set the room to rights, cleaned the blackboard, replaced the wax cones on the dictaphone and replaced some books on the shelves. The revolver and the impedimenta for the first suicide attempt she did not touch lest they might yield fingerprints or other data to interest the police whose turn it now was to evaluate the facts of the case. She took up the telephone and called Gregory to tell him about the confession of Schwarz and invite him to put things into motion. "For my part," she said, "I am going to call on Sylvie to tell her that I am back from India, and resuming her case."

But it was a distasteful prospect and she felt on the border of tears as she set forth through the pine forest in the direction of the small modern pavilion in which the girl lived – had lived for years. It was indeed her principal residence, and she had been allowed to furnish and decorate it to her own taste, so that it felt anything but clinical and austere, being decked out with brilliant hangings and old-fashioned carved furniture of heavy Second Empire beauty. It was also full of books and paintings. Her old-fashioned bed with baldaquin was set against a fine old tapestry, subdued but glowing – huntsmen with lofted horns were running down a female stag. After the rape, leaving the grooms to bring the trophy home, they galloped away into the soft brumous Italian skyline, into a network of misty lakes and romantic islets. In one corner lay the stag, panting and bleeding and in tears like a woman. Sylvie herself was not unlike the animal, but the tears had dried on her lashes and she lay in the heavy damascened bed with eyes fast shut though she was in fact awake. Moreover she knew without opening them who her visitor was. Her mind was slowly emerging from sedation to an acquaintance with sorrow and bereavement caused by

Schwarz's withdrawal from her world. "O God, my darling, so he was right; I didn't believe him when he said you would return. O my only love, my Constance! I am impatient to hear about India – O how was India, how calm was India? Constance, take my hands." She put out her own which trembled with the shock of their meeting.

Love is no respecter of persons or of contexts – it vaults every obstacle to achieve its ends. The wild spiritual attachment of Sylvie had not changed, rather it had fed on the absence of the beloved personage. Now she was trying to swallow and digest the long blank in her life for which India stood as a sort of symbol, a penitential silence on the part of Eros – for during her moments of relative sanity Schwarz had discovered that she knew as much psychoanalysis as he did: and this was a wretched enough augury for a cure and a return to ordinary life (pray, what is *that*?). It was a paradox that when she was officially mad she was often more advanced in self-understanding than at other times. So India rang out in her conversation – her only way of reforging the missing link with her adored Constance. "Has it so much changed, then? Still starving and god-drunk and spattered with dry excrement? When I was there long ago, long before you, and my love for you, I felt the moon of my non-being become full. The smell of the magnolia remembered me supremely. The deep sadness seemed very worthwhile. To be a whole person discountenanced all nature. It is different for me now that I have betrayed my brother in turning to you; I am clothed from head to foot in a marvellous seamless euphoria. In my mind your kisses clothe me close as chain-mail link by link. Only he sent you away in order to save me, but it was my ruin!"

"Now he is dead!"

"Now he is dead!"

It was as if the phrase resounding thus in echo somehow actualised the death and separation. Suddenly Constance felt weak at the knees, incoherent and shapeless, with all her joints floating with an ague. She sank down upon the bed and lay in the trusting embrace of Sylvie, aware only now of the tension of the counter-transference which she had tried to avoid by running away. The girl was kissing her with all the accurate passion of despair which was now turning to exaltation. With one part of her mind Constance was amazed at the strength of her fierce attraction for Sylvie. A whole gravitational field seemed to have grown up about this exchange, these sorrow-laden caresses. Their tears and sighs seemed to come from some vast common fund of loving sadness, and it was only when she felt her companion's hand first upon her breasts and then invading her secret parts that she came awake herself, aroused and forced to face the demons of choice. Should she allow herself to slake the love of this beautiful young stranger? And even as she asked the question she felt her own nerves respond positively, her own kisses begin to ignite under Sylvie's spell. So much for Narcissus! She was dismayed by the powerful emotions which swept her heart and only half-aware that all this was a reaction from the death of Schwarz. She had been driven out of control by it and from some depths of inner numbness had lost all power of evaluation. She was lost, washed overboard, so to speak. She clung now to the body and mind of Sylvie as if to a life-raft, happy to own this slender body, these graceful arms and slender expressive fingers. And to be loved after all she had endured was perfect heaven.

So for a brief period of time these two defeated and exhausted women would band themselves together through love and unite their strength to face an unfeeling world. In their febrile ecstasy they were become deaf to the counsels of science and reason. How intrigued Schwarz would have been to learn of this fortuitous development caused by the shock of his death and by nothing else. It was love again in one of its many disguises. Sylvie was saying, "Won't you go away now to get over it? O please take me with you! I can't bear to be left again! Take me, Constance."

And this theme too was to become an echo in the conversation of her friends – the theme of departure. After all, France was free again, although far from restored to its former glories. Sutcliffe echoed the question, and then Aubrey in his turn spelt it out. It snowballed. Lord Galen also!

The accumulated leave which Constance had coming to her spelt a whole summer and more, while Blanford was sufficiently advanced into convalescence to consider a southern holiday; Sutcliffe was waiting a posting . . . So it came about that they all met on the platform of the veteran express which served Avignon – indeed the whole eastern part of the Midi. Between them they occupied a whole section of carriage in the comfortable dining-car. "What price the *Canterbury Tales*?" said Aubrey Blanford. "The setting forth of the pilgrims, eh?" But as Sutcliffe pointed out sardonically, it was much more like an exodus of refugees. "No single complete unit like a couple, all broken up and fragmented, and in dispersion. A rebeginning of something, or an ending. This is the way that the seed leaves the sower's hand."

But Blanford's heart smote him with pain as he watched the two shy rapturous girls walking together, holding hands as they advanced along the platform, as if to give each other courage and consolation. Disgust and envy seized him, for he had been completely unprepared for this turn of events. Affad's little son – that was also a surprise, for he was delivered to the arms of Constance by the old grandmother almost without a word. Yet there were tears in her eyes as she pressed her charge forward towards Constance. The little boy went hot and cold by turns, white and red, and he clenched his fists with excitement until the knuckles were white. He had never been seized with so fierce a happiness, and the two women cherished him as if he had been their own offspring. Lord Galen was retiring to his house to mature his plans for investing in marriages of the future. Cade and Blanford were setting off side by side, living on in a state of suppressed irritation with each other and yet unable to part. Almost every day the servant remembered some new little thing about Blanford's mother – a small tesselation which enlarged the enigmatic portrait of her. Cade was sparing with these details, recognising them as part of his affectionate blackmail. Sutcliffe and Toby were supporting cast – so Toby said. They too were hoping for a restful summer in Tu Duc or Verfeuille or Meurre – they had a choice. But Sutcliffe like the others was a little plaintive. "I can't help being angry because put upon," he told Aubrey, "for, after all, what would you do if you were refused a specific and discrete identity, if you were forced to accept your role of etheric double merely, insubstantial and fantastic? Eh?"

"Better than being a product of the old button-puncher *à la* Ibsen," said Aubrey comfortably; he felt very much encouraged by this journey. "After all, Socrates was only the etheric double of Plato, he was not real so much as *true*, that is why he was so neurotic – all those fevers and fears and visions! Plato saved himself by shoving them on to Socrates' account. He was absolved from the worst by his invention. I hope you will do the same for me."

"Synaesthesia!"

"Yes."

"They will not understand."

"Nonsense! You will loom without a precise meaning like the statue in Don Giovanni, blocking the whole action, and gradually acquire symbolic weight because of your lack of personality in the human sense. Your speech is not that of a person but of an oracle."

"A semantic word – bazaar?"

"Not exactly. You will make another sort of sense in using the same sounds."

"Is semantics more antics than semen?
More suited to dons than to he-men?"

"Precisely. You win first prize, which is a battery-driven chamber-pot!"

"I shall apotheose into don."

"Cheer up, Rob. The Quinx be with you!"

"Amen!"

They sat, each following his private line of thought like a line of personal music. As for Constance, she now knew beyond a doubt, as a doctor, that man cannot do without calamity, nor can he ever circumscribe in language the inexpressible bitterness of death and separation. And love, if you wish. Love.

Cade sat somewhat apart from them all, his head bowed over his hands as he carefully pruned and buffed his large sepulchral nails. From time to time he smiled broadly and looked around him as if he dared them all to guess his thoughts.

Sutcliffe said, "And Aubrey, do you see an end to this bitter *tu quoque* – or will we go on forever?"

"They say that Socrates spent the last night on earth in silent soliloquy, alone with his Voice, so to speak."

"Inner or Outer voice?"

"Inner is Western and Outer Eastern. The Noumenon and the Phenomenon – reality turned inside out like a sleeve. It's as clear as a donkey's eyeball! Why aren't you happier?"

Lord Galen played with the stack of Order books which lay before him sheathed in rubber bands. They were full of orders for his Aids from thirsty, trusting Swiss couples. He was brooding on the marriage of the future – Adam with his great purple prick and Eve with her marsupial socket... Si vous visitez Lisbon envoyez nous un godmichet! It was prettier in English. "If you touch at Lisbon send us a dildo." It was all very well for Robin to joke ("The Swiss lover has asteroids in his underwear and spiteful hair!"), but now the war was over one must really be practical and start rebuilding the future. His couples would be anointed by computers and married by voices. In the bordel he had overheard someone say cryptically, "Elle a des sphincters d'un archimandrite Grec!" and wondered if it might have any bearing on the new devices he was fathering, the distribution of which would be controlled by the obsequious Cade as a part-time task. The whole future of marriage was an absorbing topic ("toad in the whole" – the flippant Toby with his puns got on his nerves). Lord Galen burned to serve the lovers of the future. He was hurt by the ironies of people who should have known better, like Sutcliffe: "*Mon cher*, it's going to be a case of *reculer pour mieux enculer*. We will be able to have a fuck on the NHS, with nurses specially trained by Norse fishermen for low-calibre tupping – just clickety-click and the pretty turnstile does its work. They will call it Somatotherapy."

> "Nature's fond jock-strap I taught thee to pounce
> And spiral out your orgasms ounce by ounce."

"People are so cynical," said Lord Galen to himself. "The lack of loving-kindness makes you very sad!"

Blanford was scribbling some militant verses in his commonplace book:

> Blood-gulping Christian pray take stock
> I have doffed my butcher's smock
> I have put away my cock
> Lost the key and closed the lock
> Of my passions taken stock
> Heard the ticking of time's clock
> Heard the noiseless knuckles knock
> *Toc Toc Toc   Toc Toc Toc.*

He was thinking: If we could have a summer or two of peace and quietness one might commit another novel, a votive joy, a moonshot into the future, an Indian novel. "Why not?" said his etheric double accommodatingly, "If the harvest is good and the girls beautiful enough? Why not?"

"Yesterday we devoted the whole evening to Strange Cries, Toby and I. We screamed our way into hoarseness with the macabre inventions of our fancy. We whorled and snibbed like a chapter of dervishes. Toby did the primal cry of all the nations while I toured the animal kingdom, ending up with a dog and cat fight which brought our Swiss neighbours tiptoing out on to their landings and balconies, wondering whether to call the ambulance or not. Nor did we lack invention, for after the prosaic we took to the fanciful and found sounds to illustrate abstract entities like, for example, the Magnetic Melon; some of these inventions took the skin off the Swiss mind. This morning I was in poor voice until my first drink. Last night they hammered on the door and menaced us with indignant policemen until we desisted. In the morning Toby decided to change his name to Mr Orepsorp which is only Prospero spelt backwards – though it sounds like the Welsh nickname of a man with an abbreviated foreskin. So we bade farewell to Geneva of hallowed memory, of hollow mummery."

"The *ogres* will be waiting at the station when we reach Avignon. Everything will start again when spring melts into summer. We will prune our books and re-set all the broken bones. As Dante once remarked to himself:

> See how sweet the stars are twinkling
> They have received the Greater Inkling,
> Silent, without presumptuousness
> They hang in Utter Umptiousness."

Some of these flights were to be attributed to the fine French wine served aboard the train. And while they joked the two girls sat with the little boy between them in silent rapture. Blanford thought bitterly, "L'Amour! Étrange Legume! Quel

Concerto à quatre pattes! Viens cherie, on va éplucher le concombre ensemble!"

It was grossly unfair to feel so bitter but he could not help it; ashamed, he hid in French. He was tasting the bitter fruit of sexual jealousy to the full, for he had planned to be alone with Constance. But if they were silent, the two lovers, the little boy had begun to speak as he watched the countryside spinning past them. "My father will always be watching over us from heaven. But he will not be able to come down to us except when we are asleep."

Sylvie kissed his head and squeezed his small shoulders to encourage his desire to confide in them, to relearn the freedom of speech.

"I suppose you've heard about the Prince?" said Lord Galen to Constance. "The British have arrested the entire sect on suspicion of subversive activities and the Prince just got away in the nick of time in a Red Cross plane. He is coming down to stay with me until it all blows over. I know you will be glad to see him again." It was a pleasant prospect indeed.

"If Provence is herself again we'll be able to tell, for all Spain will clamber in over the border to help with the grape-harvest. Spanish girls among the vines with names like Conception and Incarnation and Revaluation and Revelation."

"Not to mention Infibulation and Abomination and Peroration and Inflation and Deflagration and . . . Phlogiston."

"How 'Phlogiston'?"

"Just Phlogiston!"

"Not to mention Adumbration, Marination and Abominable Secretion!"

"The harvest is assured. As for me, I shall be thinking about the title for my autobiography. How about *Last Will and Testicle* or *Parallel People* or *Catch as Catch Can't* or *Out First Ball* or *Options, Inklings and other Involuntary Chuckles?*"

Cade poured out the wine. The train flew on.